T.N.T.

Spur heard a noise and looked up. The robber was on top of the rock less than six feet away! Spur lifted the Winchester and fired. The unaimed round skidded off the stone breaking up and splattering some of its hot lead into the robber who dropped out of sight.

"Don't be a fool," Spur called. "You're hurt and I'll kill you if I have to, just like I did Varner. You ready to die?"

There was no answer.

A stick of dynamite with a short fuse sailed over to the granite boulder and Spur dove away from it, rolling as far as he could toward the open space behind the rock.

The blast went off with a cracking roar.

Also in the SPUR Series:

SPUR #20

COLORADO CUTIE

LEISURE BOOKS ❧ NEW YORK CITY

A LEISURE BOOK

Published by

Dorchester Publishing Co., Inc.
6 East 39th Street
New York, N.Y. 10016

Printed in the United States of America

COLORADO CUTIE

1

Two black horses thundered out of the side street, their eyes wild, foam flying from their mouths as the desperados on their backs spurred them viciously. The men fired deadly six-guns at anyone who moved on the small Kansas town's Main Street as they pulled up at the Newtown bank.

Two other bank robbers inside the venerable establishment burst through the big doors carrying carpetbags stuffed with all the paper money in the safe and tellers' cages. The second pair of ne'er-do-wells leaped on board waiting chargers and emptied pistols at the men from the bank, and others foolhardy enough to oppose them.

"If any of my men are wounded, I'll come back and kill every man in town!" the leader roared. The man on the silver gray stallion was Big Red Ryerson, the scourge of the plains, the most wanted bank robber in a dozen states, and now taking his deadly toll on this small Kansas town of no more than two thousand souls.

Sheriff Johnny White pushed his hat back on his head from where he crouched beside the hardware store, his Remington repeating rifle at the ready. Slowly he lowered the rifle. He would not endanger the men of the town by shooting up the bank robbers now. He would wait until they were well out of town, then with a selected posse he would throw down on them while they camped, and capture every man without spilling any blood.

The outlaws laughed and shot out two store windows as they thundered out of town, making Sheriff Johnny White look like a coward in the eyes of the citizens of Newtown. Johnny didn't worry about that, he could live with criticism until he brought Big Red Ryerson to justice.

But he hoped that Caroline Caruthers did not think ill of him. She was the prairie flower he loved, and soon he was going to tell her.

Sheriff Johnny White ran into Main Street, fired three shots into the air.

"All right, the town is safe now. I need six volunteers who can shoot straight to form a posse. Who is with me?"

Willard Kleaner looked up from the short story he had been reading. Wow! There were the men, that was the action he thought he would find in the West. The pages of *Amazing Western Stories* told what the Wild West was really like! He'd read every one he could find when he could talk his father out of a dime.

But his father had been killed in a runaway buggy six months ago and now Willard was here in Johnson Corners, Colorado living with his Aunt and Uncle. But this *couldn't be the West!* Nothing was the same. He hadn't seen a single Indian. There were no big herds of buffalo, and the only cowboys he had seen were short, dirty, foul-mouthed and about as colorful as a slab of brown bread.

This couldn't be the Wild West!

Willard looked out from the porch of a clapboard house where he sat reading the dime western. He was fifteen years old, had finished the eighth grade of regular school and one year of higher school in Chicago. He was tall and new-corn thin, with a mop of carrot red hair, dark green eyes and a face full of freckles.

He'd had a fight for every one of his freckles and had won most of them. Now he stared in silent anger at the poor excuse of a real Western town that cluttered along the main street. They called it Johnson Corners. Now wasn't that a colorful name for a western town!

His uncle, who ran one of two small hotels in town, said there were over two thousand people in town and the surrounding valley.

"Yes sir, Willard," his Uncle Ronald Lewton said. "We're building something good here. Johnson Corners is going to be a big town someday. We're not a hundred miles from Denver, and we get a lot of traffic through here along the trail west. We've got a good bit of cattle ranching already, and being so close to the railroad, we'll do right fine with farm products too.

"This is a town to grow in, to grab opportunity and shake it by the throat and beat a living out of it. Right here in Johnson Corners!"

Willard sighed. He put his finger in the dime novel and tried to imagine Big Red Ryerson thundering around the corner on his horse, shooting out the windows in the stores, robbing the bank and laughing as he rode out.

When he opened his eyes, Big Red Ryerson was well out of town, the sheriff was chasing him, and Willard wondered if he had been born twenty years too late. Here it was 1877 and most of the Wild West wasn't all that wild anymore. If he'd only been here back in the mid sixties! Right after the Civil War, before the railroad came! That would have been the really great time.

Willard could almost imagine it. Only pockets of people, a few fences, lots of horses and cattle and buffalo. Those would have been the days! He would have been a foreman on a cattle ranch, where he could ride and rope, and make trail drives down to the rail head in Kansas.

Yeah! He couldn't even ride a horse. Maybe he could get a job as a swamper down at the livery and learn to ride there. He'd ask his uncle.

"Willard!" a thin, whinish voice came from the parlor. "Willard, it's time you were getting to the hotel if'n you want your allowance. Nobody gets paid around this house for sitting on his fanny all morning."

"Yes, Aunt Zelda. I'm leaving right now."

His aunt's thin, frowning face appeared behind the front screen door staring down at him.

"Willard, be sure to leave that horrible dime novel here. I don't want anyone decent seeing you reading that trash. The very idea!"

"Yes, ma'am," he said. He held the soft paper dime novel as far as the door when his aunt whipped it out of his hand.

"Had my way I'd burn this for kindling." She sniffed. "But your uncle says its little enough we can do." Her scowl deepened. "Lord knows we try."

"Yes, ma'am. I'll be going now."

Willard hurried off the porch, anxious to get out of

the sound of her irritating voice. Willard knew that his father had left him some money when he died. He didn't know how much, or where it was. His uncle was his legal guardian now, but the money was in a "trust" whatever that was. But his uncle did get twenty dollars a month to pay for "food, clothing and shelter" for Willard's keep.

William knew that twenty dollars a month was more than some working men made. That was two hundred and forty dollars a year! What he could do with that much money!

Still his uncle said he had to work around the hotel to help pay his keep. He did get fifteen cents a day for every day he worked cleaning the hotel, working in the laundry and mopping down the hallways.

As Willard came around the corner into Main Street, he saw the stage pulling in. He ran. The stage came twice a day, east toward Chicago in the afternoon, and west toward Denver in the morning. The arrival of the stage was usually the most exciting event to take place in Johnson Corners on any day.

The big Concord coach rolled along like a prairie schooner, rocking on the heavy leather straps that helped absorb some of the jolts of the roadway. The Concord was the biggest and best of the stage coaches, and William was fascinated by them.

He ran now, caught up with the coach and trotted alongside it as the team of six began to slow so the rig could stop exactly in front of the Overland Express office.

Willard checked out the big coach to see if it was one of the new ones. He knew a lot about the big coaches. Most of them weighed more than a ton, stood eight feet high and often cost as much as $1,500 to buy. They could carry as many as twenty-one passengers—nine seated inside and the rest hanging on while sitting on the roof.

The driver's box up front was usually shared by an express company messenger riding shotgun over his often precious cargo. Under the driver's box was the boot, a leather covered area that held mail and express items and a strongbox with valuables. Personal baggage and larger express parcels were carried in another leather enclosed boot in the rear.

A Concord might use four or six horses, depending on the hills that had to be climbed. Most Concords that wheeled into Johnson Corners came with six.

Willard looked with interest and saw that this Concord had the two throughbraces, the three-inch strips of leather that served as shock absorbers for the ride. The writer Mark Twain said the straps made the coach ride like a cradle on wheels.

For a moment the coach outdistanced Willard, so he ran faster, caught up and then had to stop quickly as the driver put on the hand brake on the big rear wheels and the Concord from the Ben Holiday Overland Express Company came to a sudden halt at the express office.

Willard moved back against the side of the building and watched in open amazement as the stableman rushed forward and unhitched the six horses. Helpers led them down the alley and brought back six fresh horses for the run on toward Denver.

He fantasized himself hitching up the horses, backing them into the tongue, then hitching the second pair and the third in front of them. Black leather harness shining, the steel connectors sturdy and sure.

Then he would trade places with the driver and go dashing out of town, eager to get his cargo and passengers into Denver where there would be a layover for a good night's rest and some fine food.

Willard turned and watched the passengers getting off. Some might even be staying. A woman with red hair stepped down, looked around, saw him and waved. Willard wasn't sure she waved at him, he didn't know her. When she laughed and pointed to a big suitcase that the shotgun guard lifted off the top of the rig for her, he turned away.

He watched the next person get off, a tall man with a moustache and sandy brown sideburns well below his ears. The man wore town clothes, a brown suit and white shirt with a black string tie. He carried a battered brown hat with a low crown and a row of Spanish silver coins as a headband.

Willard knew at once that the man was a famous outlaw. One look at the six-gun worn low and tied down to his thigh proved to Willard that he had been right. Nobody in town wore his holster tied down that way. A gunsharp!

Maybe they would have a shoot-out!

Maybe a call-out and a gun duel on Main Street!

Maybe a bank robbery by the man and his gang of cutthroats who steal horses and thunder out of town shooting out the store windows and . . .

The man he had been watching motioned to him.

"Son, could you take my bag over to the best hotel in town? I'm thirsty and can't wait to lift a beer or two."

The tall stranger dropped a medium sized carpetbag at his feet and stared down at Willard.

"Son?" the stranger said.

"Huh? Oh, yes sir. Sorry, I was thinking . . ."

"Could you take my bag over to the hotel? Give it to the desk clerk and tell him I'll register when I get there. My name is Spur McCoy."

"Yes, sir! You bet," Willard said. He wanted to ask him if he were really a gunsharp, a fast gun, an outlaw maybe! But Willard simply nodded and picked up the bag. He had taken two steps toward the Aspen Hotel when the man called.

"Hey, son."

Willard stopped and turned. The man tossed a coin at him and Willard caught it smoothly. It was a quarter!

"Here's something for your trouble. Tell the clerk that bag better be there when I come or he's in for some trouble. What's your name, son?"

"Willard, sir. Willard Kleaner. I work at the Aspen Hotel. Your bag will be there."

The tall man nodded, turned and watched the red-headed woman talking to the shotgun guard for a moment, then walked quickly across the street to the biggest drinking establishment he could see on Main Street, the Evangeline Saloon and Gaming House.

Spur McCoy saw the sign of the Aspen Hotel half a block down the dirt street of Johnson Corners, waved at the young redheaded boy, and walked with a thirsty purpose across the street, avoiding the horse droppings. He stepped up to the boardwalk built in front of the business establishments and pushed through the swinging doors into the Evangeline Saloon.

He was interested in a cold beer or two to start, then he would check in at the hotel and have a late midday meal. When he came back to the saloon he might try his hand at some poker. It had been some time since he had indulged himself with the pasteboards.

As soon as he stepped inside the Evangeline he knew it was a different kind of saloon. The floor was clean, oiled and well scrubbed. More than a dozen coal oil lamps already lighted the place with twenty more hanging ready to be lit. The chairs and poker tables were in good repair, varnished and orderly.

The voices were subdued and he didn't notice any men wearing guns. He had a quick look at a woman who stepped from behind the bar and vanished into a rear room. There were no dance hall girls in sight.

A huge man four inches taller than Spur's six-foot two inches, stopped three feet from Spur. He had a barrel chest, arms the size of railroad ties and looked as if he carried 280 pounds of solid muscle.

He looked straight into Spur's eyes.

"Miss Evangeline asks you to check your six-gun," the man said in a surprisingly soft voice.

Spur looked around and saw now that none of the men wore gunbelts. He shrugged.

"Why not?" he said, and took off his leather and the .45 with the long barrel and handed it to the big man who gave him a poker chip with a number written on it.

When Spur turned toward the bar, the woman was there again. He smiled automatically and stepped up to the polished mahogany that glistened even in the lamplight. The only thing Spur saw was the woman behind the bar. She was short, delicately formed with soft brown hair on her shoulders and a alabaster complexion with two dimples and a pair of darting black eyes.

Spur smiled. She smiled back and he saw the heavy gold chain around her neck outside the chin high white blouse. The chain had in the center the largest pearl Spur had ever seen.

"You must be Miss Evangeline," Spur said.

She smiled again and the dimples deepened. The pretty woman nodded slightly. "True, and you must be Spur McCoy. You look thirsty, how about a cold beer?"

2

Spur McCoy was jolted when the beautiful bar maid called him by name. He had never been in this small Colorado town before. From long practice, he had not shown surprise at the woman's use of his name.

"That's right kindly of you, miss. I certainly could use a cold beer. Ice house?"

"Sam built a big one at the edge of town and supplies us all summer. Lower his supply gets, higher the price." She opened a bottle of beer and pushed it toward him, her dark eyes curious.

"You didn't seem surprised when I called you by name. Why?"

Spur grinned, tipped the bottle and took a long pull. When he let it down he wiped his mouth and looked at her. "Are you always so outspoken, so direct?"

"Usually, unless I'm playing poker, then you won't ever know what I'm thinking."

"Sounds like an interesting gamble."

"You are interested to find out how I knew your

name, I can tell. But you didn't let on, not even a flicker of an eyebrow. So, that makes you a railroad agent, or maybe a Pinkerton, or just possibly a U.S. Marshal. Now that we're a state I don't know if the U.S. Marshals work around here.''

"They do, but I'm not one." He pulled at the beer again. "That tastes good after eating dust for forty miles. And it's served by the prettiest lady I've seen in town.''

She pouted for a moment, lips thrust out, eyes almost closed, chin up. Then she laughed, "Sir, that is no compliment, since you just got off the stage and the only woman you've seen is our redheaded Lotty, who is one of our town's few ladies of ill repute.''

"Lotty is not much of a talker. She didn't say three words to anybody on the stage.''

"Lotty has other talents and skills.''

Spur chuckled. "I would guess. Now, I am curious. Are you Evangeline?''

"Guilty. I own the place and run it straight and clean. No house rules, no cheating, no gunplay. Every card dealt comes off a deck laid flat on the table. Haven't even had a fist fight in here in six months.''

Spur finished the beer and pushed the bottle back to her. She took it and put it below the bar. It was a little before noon but already four poker tables were busy.

Spur had a dozen questions for her, but he also was hungry, felt grimy from the long ride, and wanted a bath. He tipped his hat and pushed back from the long bar.

"I'll count on talking to you later," he said.

"Anytime, McCoy. I'm always here." She smiled and both dimples popped in. "I'll look forward to our next little chat.''

Spur collected his gun belt and iron from the big man near the door and walked into the sunshine. It was high country in the Rocky Mountains, the air clear and crisp, the sun beaming down warm, and at night the stars so close you could reach up and play jacks with them.

The town had about two thousand people, Washington had told him. The man he looked for couldn't be too hard to find. But there was a curious proviso in his orders. He'd go over them carefully when he got into his room.

Spur dropped off the boardwalk and into the dust of the street, dodged one farm wagon with the driver already asleep, counting on the team of horses to take him safely back to his ranch. The team probably knew the way better than he did.

On the far boardwalk he passed the Weber Brothers Clothing House and the McNamara Bakery. Then came Bill Johnson Groceries before he reached the Aspen Hotel. Spur went up the six steps to the lobby. Three old men sat in chairs on the small front porch. They nodded at him and he waved back, then walked inside.

The redheaded boy he had seen in the street was sweeping the lobby. The youngster nodded and kept sweeping. At the desk Spur gave his name and the clerk's interest picked up slightly when he saw Spur in a town suit.

"Yes, sir, Mr. McCoy. We've put you in Two-C, right in front and just down from the stairs."

"Good. I'd also like a bath. Do you have separate bathrooms or do I get a tub brought to my room?"

"Sir, we have a bath on each floor. You'll be just across from the bath on two. I'll have some big towels sent up. Will there by anything else you need?"

18

Spur shook head, signed the register and gave the man six dollars for six nights.

"There is a fifty cent charge for the bathwater," the clerk said apologetically.

"Best half a dollar I ever spent," Spur said, took the key and walked up the open stairs to the second floor.

Inside Two-C he found his carpetbag on the bed. He checked carefully but it had not been opened. Before he had his bag unpacked and into the small dresser, a knock sounded on his door. Spur touched his Colt .45 on his hip and walked without a sound to the door. He pulled it open suddenly.

A young woman stood there with two large, fluffy white towels over her arm. She was sturdily built with broad shoulders, long blonde hair and large breasts pushing against a white blouse she had outgrown.

Brown eyes evaluated him as she grinned. "You wanted some towels for a bath?"

"Yes, thanks."

"I'll put them in the bathroom for you. Willard has already brought up the hot water. Better hurry before it gets cold." She smiled at him and walked toward the bath down one room and across the hall. He could see the smooth operation of her hips under the skirt.

Spur closed the door. Now there was a healthy young woman, who would not try too hard to chase away a man. For just a moment he thought about his orders. He should check them again. Gen. Halleck had told him in a wire to proceed to Johnson Corners, Colorado and determine if one Horace Olson was in town. He was reported to be living here under the name of George Slocum. He was about thirty-five and was wanted in Washington D.C. for murder and counterfeiting.

Spur pulled off his jacket, and his tie. He took a stack of clothes he would put on and walked to the bathroom. The door was ajar and inside he saw three steaming buckets of water as well as one that was probably cold.

Spur closed the door and began taking off his shirt. Before he could react, soft woman's hands reached around his chest and helped him undo the buttons. Then he felt her press against his back, her breasts warm, her hot breath on his neck.

"Thought you might need some help with your bath," she said. She slid around until she was in front of him. The white blouse was unbuttoned and pulled out of the dark skirt. Soft white flesh showed through the opening and the blush of a pink areola on one breast.

She grinned up at him. "I'm Tessie, Spur McCoy, and I'd just love to scrub your back."

She watched his face for a moment. The first surprise had been replaced by a smile and she reached up and kissed his cheek.

"I don't give just anybody this kind of special service," Tessie said. "Maybe we better lock the door." She moved away from him, threw the bolt on the bathroom door and when she turned she took off the white blouse.

Her breasts were high, full, with bright red, thumb-sized nipples on discs of pink areolas. Tessie shook her shoulders so her breasts bounced and jiggled.

"I don't want to get my blouse wet while I scrub you," she said. "We better get the water in the tub before it goes cold." She lifted the first bucket and emptied it into the tub, then the other two hot ones. She put her hand in the water and pulled it back quickly. Tessie dumped in half the bucket of cold and smiled.

"Bath time, Spur, now don't be bashful. It may be hard to believe, but I actually have seen a man's good parts all bare and hard!"

"You are serious, aren't you?"

"Hey! I don't show my titties to just anybody." She covered her eyes a moment with a hand. "But you're about the most handsome man I've ever seen. And I don't mind washing backs . . . or fronts for that matter."

She moved up to him and finished undoing his shirt buttons and pulling it off him.

"Yes, lots of black chest hair! I like some hair on a man's broad chest, helps cover up his man titties." She reached in and kissed both the buds on his chest.

"Now, the pants. You gonna wear a gunbelt when you're soaking in the big tub?"

The tub was one of the new ones, almost six feet long, and made of heavy, nickel plated metal, and had four sturdy claw legs.

Tessie pulled off his gunbelt and opened his fly.

"Oh, yes, the good stuff!" she shrilled. She tugged down his pants and then the short underwear and sat back on her heels in surprise. "Lordy, lordy, lordy! Would you look at him!"

Tessie bent quickly, kissed his throbbing erection, then took off his boots and the rest of his clothes and led him to the tub.

"In you go, and save room for me!"

Spur stepped into the tub of hot water and gingerly sat down. As he did, Tessie stripped out of her dark skirt and the drawers she wore that came to her knee. She stood there naked for a minute watching him, then stepped in the tub and sat down in the steaming water facing him.

"Watch out where you put your toes!" she said and they both broke up laughing. They both grabbed wash cloths and bars of soap and sudsed each other seriously. Spur used only his hands to wash her breasts and Tessie rolled her eyes and grabbed through the water at his crotch.

"That does me furious fast that way!" she panted. She pulled Spur down in the tub until she could straddle his crotch, then held the sides of the tub and lowered herself toward him.

"You're gonna have to aim that lance of yours, sweetie!" she said. Spur adjusted and with a groan felt her lower onto his throbbing penis.

"Oh, glory!" Tessie squealed. "I never done it this way before. Just glorious!" She began lifting herself by the sides of the tub and dropping back on his turgid member. A dozen drops and Spur was thrusting upward in the water to meet her. Their union was under the water now and waves threatened to break over the top of the tub on each stroke.

Tessie's face turned red and her breathing was so fast and ragged she sounded like a panting steam engine.

"Do me! Do me!" she rumbled. "Oh, damn! Oh shit! Oh fuck! That is so wonderful! I've never been touched like that inside before. Oh glory! I'm dead and done gone to heaven for sure. No fucking has ever been so marvelous, so great, so fucking wonderful!"

Tessie shrieked then and Spur brought his hand over her mouth to hold down the sound. Her face turned purple as her whole body shook and rattled and vibrated as she kept dropping again and again on Spur's lance. He met her quickened strokes and just before she fell forward on top of him, he reached his own climax and jolted upward until his breath billowed out in raw steam. He thrust her naked form a foot off the bath tub.

Tessie lay against Spur's chest, her legs around his waist and in back of him. For a moment he wondered if she had died or only fainted.

Then Tessie giggled.

"Glory, we done fucked in the bathwater!"

"About the size of it," Spur said. He eased her away from him to a sitting position.

"Going, going . . . gone," Tessie said. "You just deserted me."

"He has a way of coming down to size after an outing," Spur said.

"Otherwise you'd have trouble walking!" Tessie laughed and pulled away from him. She used the cloth and washed him off and then herself and stepped out of the tub and brought the two fluffy towels.

"When I came to your door, you didn't get any ideas about doing me?" she asked.

"Ideas? Most men, from time to time, look at a pretty, sexy girl and wonder what it would be like. But wondering is usually as far as it gets."

"Did you wonder about me?"

"Yes, especially that tightly filled white blouse."

"My best features. I mean every girl's got one between her legs, but nobody can see that. Tits are right up there and if a girl's got them, it's a lot easier."

They began drying themselves with the big towels.

"You like making love, Tessie?"

"Oh, yes! Who doesn't? Girls I know who have done it, like it, unless they got raped the first time or it was bad. Sex is great. Part of the fun of working here. I get first look at the most handsome men who come to town. Once I flirted with this young guy and he didn't give me a glance. So that night I unlocked his door and slipped naked into his bed. When he finally woke up I had him half inside and he couldn't stop. That was a wild one the rest of the night. He couldn't get enough once he got started."

Spur put on his clothes, a brown western plaid shirt and jeans.

"What happens when you get pregnant?"

"Lordy, I worry about that if it happens. I talked to the doc and he said there are ways. I do him now and then, kind of in payment for his services. He told me ways. Like right after the curse is over is the best time."

Tessie put on her drawers and her skirt, then stood there near him bare topped.

"You like my titties?"

Spur stroked each one, then kissed them and she groaned.

"Let's do one more, right here on the floor!"

Spur laughed and stepped to the door with his clothes. "Tessie, maybe later, right now I have to go and get some business done."

"What business you in, McCoy?"

"Business. I'm looking for a small business to buy. Might stay in town."

"Good, let's do this again."

Spur smiled. "Never can tell, Tessie. Just never can tell. Say, you might know a man I need to see, George Slocum."

Tessie laughed. "Why you want to see him, you get the crotch itch or something? I didn't give you nothing. George is the guy I was talking about before. George is the town's only doctor."

3

Spur watched Tessie closely. She was telling the truth. The man he had come to find was the town's only doctor. That would make arresting him ten times as hard. He'd seen whole towns close ranks behind a doctor and lie like Indian squaws to keep the man in town.

Spur opened the bathroom door, carrying his travel weary clothes and smiled. "You asked why I have to see Doc Slocum. Same as the rest of it, just business." He winked. "You take care of those twin beauties, you hear?"

A few moments later McCoy closed his door and dropped the clothes on the bed. Time to start laying his cover story. He combed his hair, trimmed his moustache and shaved fresh, then went down to the first good sized store and went in to talk to the owner.

Before closing time at six p.m., he had canvassed six stores. None of them were for sale, but one couple was willing to listen to a price. By morning every merchant in town would know he was there with the idea of buying out an existing business. Then he would be able to get down to his real work.

He had a quick, uneventful meal at the Aspen Hotel dining room and discovered it was not going to be the best place in town to eat. Upstairs in his room he lit a coal oil lamp, put it on the dresser and lounged on the bed reading a telegram from his boss in Washington D.C.

Spur McCoy was a United States Secret Service Agent, working directly under the command of Gen. William D. Halleck. The general gave the orders for the number one man, William Wood, the director of the agency appointed by President Lincoln and reappointed by each succeeding president.

Spur opened the telegram he had picked up in Denver and read it again.

McCOY. PROCEED TO JOHNSON CORNERS, COL. LOCATE AND DETAIN ONE GEORGE SLOCUM. SAID TO BE RESIDING THERE UNDER THAT ALIAS. WANTED FOR MURDER AND COUNTERFEITING. MAY BE DANGEROUS. ARREST SLOCUM, TRANSPORT HIM TO THE FEDERAL COURTHOUSE IN DENVER FOR ARRAIGNMENT AND TRANSFER TO WASH. D.C. FOR TRIAL. SPECIAL CIRCUMSTANCES: WE HAVE NO HARD INFORMATION ON THIS SUSPECT. WHAT WE KNOW COMES FROM AN INFORMANT. INVESTIGATE CAREFULLY BEFORE TAKING ACTION.

REPORT PROGRESS WHEN POSSIBLE,

AND REPORT DISPOSITION WHEN THE CASE IS FINISHED.

The orders had come addressed to Spur McCoy, Investigator, Capital Investigations Inc. at the Denver Overland stage office. His trip here by stage had been difficult, tiring but spectacular visually along the rim of the highest mountains in the nation. Now he stared again at the seemingly contradictory parts of his orders. One said bring Slocum in for trial, the other paragraph said go easy, be careful, this might not be the right man.

The saloon lady might have some information on his man, if he went about it right. Spur changed shirts, put on a pair of town pants and a brown leather vest, string tie and his new brown low crowned hat and headed for Evangeline's.

There was still a half hour to sundown when Spur came out the hotel door. The same redheaded boy who had carried his bag to the hostelry, sat on the steps. When he saw Spur, he jumped and walked toward him.

He came slowly at first, then when Spur glanced at him he pushed out his chin and strode ahead with determination. When he was six feet away, the youngster's steps slowed, his face worked and he frowned for a minute.

Then he blurted out what must have been thought out and rehearsed.

"Mr. McCoy. Are you really a United States Marshal the way folks say you are?"

"Well, now, Willard, who says that?"

"The desk clerk. He said it. You are a lawman, ain't you, since you got a tied down gun and all?"

Spur smiled and shook his head. "Sorry, Willard,

I'm not a U.S. Marshal. I'm a businessman, here to look for a good opportunity. You know of any?"

Willard frowned and took half a step back. "Well, no I don't, Mr. McCoy, but I'm just a kid."

"A kid? Out West kids grow up in a rush. How old are you, fourteen?"

"Most fifteen and a half, Mr. McCoy."

"See what I mean? Western boys get to be men at near sixteen."

"But I'm from Chicago. Only been here in Johnson Corners for a month now."

"Don't matter, Willard. You're almost a man. Now, I got one more business call. Oh, your dad run the hotel?"

"No, sir, Mr. McCoy. My father's dead. That's my uncle who owns the Aspen."

"Oh, I'm sorry. Well, Willard, I have one more business call to make."

Spur continued across the boardwalk and into the dust of the street.

Willard watched him go. He figured Spur McCoy was at least six feet and two inches, maybe two hundred pounds. And his gun was tied low on his right thigh. It reminded him of the story about Forty-Four Jones in *Lonesome Rider on Dead Sage Mesa.*

Now there was a man! But Spur McCoy looked just as good. Tall, and lean with powerful shoulders and that deadly six-gun.

Willard walked along the street for half a block before he turned down to go to his uncle's house. He was reliving the shootout at the south range water trough from the current Western dime novel he was reading, when he went past the alley in back of the Main Street businesses.

It was getting dusk now. Half light could affect the way a person saw things, but Willard knew for certain that there were two men on horses in the alley. That was a bit strange. Most men hitched their nags at the front of the store. There were only a few houses that backed up to the alley from the other street.

Willard faded behind an aspen tree growing near the alley and waited, watching in the long dark strip. He knew there were two desperados in there waiting to rob some saloon! Or maybe planning a bank robbery! Yes. The Concord State Bank was on that block!

Willard could almost see the men.

Then he did, as two men came walking their horses from the alley directly toward him. He froze in his boots.

The men came from the alley and turned toward Main Street, failing to see him, but Willard had a good look at them.

The first one led a gray with a saddle and saddle bags and a Remington Repeating rifle in the boot. He had a bedroll and another sack for grub tied in back of his saddle. The pair had just come in from a long ride.

The first man was in his twenties, Willard guessed. He was clean shaven except for a moustache that drooped around his mouth and gave off twisted strands two inches longer that had been waxed and nurtured. He wore one of those long coats that outlaws used to hide their shotguns under!

The second man led a black. He had a dark crushed hat with almost no crown, a swarthy face under a full beard. He wore what almost looked like a Rebel officer's coat and he walked as if his feet hurt. He was much taller than the first man.

Willard turned and watched the pair go past the lamplight coming out the saloon on the corner. Both were desperados, he knew! Should he run back and try to find Mr. McCoy and tell him that bank robbers were in town?

Willard turned and shuffled slowly toward his uncle's house. No, he couldn't tell Mr. McCoy, although Willard was sure the man was a peace officer of some kind. The tied low gun proved that. Only lawmen and outlaws wore guns that way, and it was plain that Mr. McCoy was no outlaw, gambler, gunsharp or robber.

The first week Willard had been in town he thought for sure he saw a killing take place and he'd run to the sheriff and led him back to the alley, but it was only two drunks shooting at whiskey bottles. The sheriff rawhided him good about that.

Willard's head sagged as he came closer to his uncle's house. Maybe he wasn't cut out to be a Westerner. Maybe all this reading he was doing had turned his head around.

Willard scowled at a mulberry tree. Danged if he was going to believe that! No sir! He could be just as good at being a Westerner as anybody. He'd learn to ride and rope and even shoot a gun when he could afford to buy one!

He'd have his own horse and saddle and even spurs!

Willard walked into his uncle's house with his head high and more sure now than ever that he *had* seen two bank robbers slipping into town. Maybe he could find Mr. McCoy and at least report the chance that the men were robbers.

Yes, that sounded like a good plan. It was the way young Billy Roberts handled that problem he had in *Death Rides The Range*. It worked for Billy.

Willard let the screen door slam as he entered the house. It was June and plenty warm even in the evening.

"Willard! When on earth are you going to learn not to let that screen door slam? You know how it hurts my head. Sometimes I think you do it just to aggravate me."

The voice came from the parlor, where Willard knew his Aunt Zelda sat in the rocker fanning herself and nipping at a bottle of wine. She said it was medicine for her bad back, but he knew better.

"Sorry, Aunt Zelda, I forgot. I'll go right up to my room."

"You have supper, boy?"

"Yes, ma'am. Uncle Ron and I ate in his office."

"Well, all right. See to it that you don't read those horrid dime novels all night. I threw that one away, but you probably have more. Don't bother about me, I'll be fine."

Willard heard the start of the slurred words. She would be unconscious in the rocker by the time his uncle Ron came home. They certainly were a strange couple. Not at all like his parents had been.

Willard went up the steps quietly, so Aunt Zelda would not hear and call to him again. He was still wondering about the two bank robbers. Should he tell Mr. McCoy about them or not? He would have to figure it out by the time he went to work tomorrow morning. What should he do?

McCoy had worn his six-gun out of habit as he left the hotel, now he took off the leather and handed it to the big man inside the front door of Evangeline's. The saloon was not only kept clean, it was well appointed, with decorations and even oil paintings on the walls that Spur was sure most of the men never noticed, let alone appreciated.

The place was almost full. All of the poker tables were busy, with men waiting for empty chairs. A game of black-jack thrived at the end of the bar. Two men with white aprons around their waists hoisted beers behind the bar and poured an occasional whiskey.

Evangeline was not to be seen.

Spur ordered a beer and watched the crowd. No women, not even dance hall girls. Evangeline ran a pristine clean operation. She probably didn't even cut the whiskey.

He turned to look down the bar the other way and found her standing beside him.

Evangeline was not a dazzler, rather she was a presence, a picture of everyone's mother, daughter, sweetheart. Her soft brown hair swirled around her shoulders and for a moment her dimples popped in.

"I wondered when you were coming back for our talk," she said softly with just a hint of concern in her gentle voice.

"Would now be a good time?"

She smiled and dimpled. They held in place. Her delicate features softened, and she nodded.

"I know the management and have a reserved table." She turned and led the way through the poker players and wheels of chance to a raised platform near the back of the saloon. On the two foot high mesa sat a carved black walnut table with a snow white cloth on it decorated with lace. A single white candle sat on top near a slender vase that held one red rose.

Fragile leaded glass stemware for two rested on the linen cloth. They stepped up and he held the chair for her. It was a fine dining room chair to match the small table. He sat across from her and as he sat down, one of the barmen brought a bottle of champagne and opened it. He set the bottle beside Spur and left.

"Now we talk," Evangeline said. "To answer your question, I do have a last name, but few here remember it. I came to town almost seven years ago with my husband Frederick. He was a gambler, and a good one. He won this saloon in a game of five card stud.

"We fixed it up, cleaned it up, renamed it, and made it into the best gaming house in town. Then one night Frederick took on the Pascal brothers in a poker game. He beat them both, and as he scraped in the last pot, one of the brothers shot him with a hideout derringer. That's why I don't allow any guns in my saloon."

She watched him as he poured the champagne. It was imported from France.

"Now, who is Spur McCoy, and why are you here?"

Spur chuckled and lit a thin black cheroot. He sucked in a mouthful of smoke and then blew it out slowly.

"You are one of the most direct people I've ever met. Which is surprising but not unpleasant. I'm a businessman. My father has several stores in New York City and does importing, but I wanted something a little less hectic, where there was less pressure. So I came west."

Evangeline swirled the champagne in her tall stem glass and then sipped at it. "Then it is true, you are here looking for a business to buy."

"Or I might start one if nothing touches my fancy." He smiled at her and stared around. "I must say that I am totally amazed at this place. You know the reputations most saloons have, the rougher, the more fights the better. A killing a day keeps the whiskey flowing. You take a different approach."

"And it works. After my husband died I swore I would never let guns in here again. I sent the three fancy ladies packing and did a lot of construction and redecorating and put in absolutely honest gaming tables. If I catch one of my dealers or operators cheating, I tar and feather him and run him down Main Street."

"It seems to work. Are you filled this way every night?"

"Most of the time. If it thins out, I'll bring in a woman singer. They come out of Denver now and then. A good one can boost profits tremendously. But right now I don't need that kind of trouble."

Voices raised two tables over. Spur looked around as two men leaped to their feet glaring at each other. Spur never saw her move but the next moment tiny Evangeline stood between the two big cowboys and in her hand was a short whip with burs in the tails of the nine strips of leather.

She cracked the whip on the top of the table sending chips and paper money flying. The two angry men stared at each other a moment. Then both stopped yelling and looked at the small woman between them.

Evangeline said something that Spur couldn't hear and the men shot angry glances toward each other. She talked to them a moment longer and slowly both men sat down at the table, the chips were arranged, and Evangeline stood beside the table as the rest of the hand was played out. There was no sign of the whip.

When a new hand had been dealt, the proprietor came back to the elevated table. Spur poured fresh champagne for her after he seated her at the fancy table.

"You should be a diplomat. We could use you in Washington, or maybe France."

"I don't like France, it's too damp and wintry. At least here we have three months of warm weather."

"Were you a diplomat in France?"

"No, my father was. They don't let ten year olds be ambassadors." She paused, sipped at the wine, then her darting black eyes looked up at him. "Have you found a business you like here yet?"

"Just starting. I did see a sign that I must have read wrong. Did it say Doctor Slocum? Could that be George Slocum?"

"Yes. Doc Slocum. Do you know him from somewhere else?"

"Must be a different man. One I knew wasn't even a doctor. Has he been in town long?"

"He was here when we came through and decided to stay. He's good with the bedside manner, but he says he doesn't do operations any more."

"Must be a different man. I don't want to buy a doctor's practice anyway. Do you know of any businesses in town that are for sale, and what's the best way to make a living in this small community?"

As he said it Spur reminded himself to get some local greenbacks to check. Once a counterfeiter, always a counterfeiter. It was a tough habit to break. He'd check some local bills to see if there was any funny money around.

4

Evangeline took out a deck of cards from a drawer in the table and began shuffling. She knew how to handle cards.

"Want to play some twenty-one while we talk?" she asked.

"The way you work those cards?"

"No money to change hands." She dealt a hand of twenty-one and beat him with two cards. She won five out of the first six hands.

"See what I mean, you're a real gambler, Evangeline, I'm just a beginner."

She smiled and her dark eyes tracked him. "For now. You could be setting me up for later. What kind of a business are you looking for, retail, service, banking? We could do with a better bank in town, that's for sure. Bart Concord knows almost nothing about banking. I don't see how he makes a go of it. But he does."

"I'm not the banker type. How's the livery stable?"

"First rate, and room for just one. Be hard to compete with Josh."

"Could I get some change, Evangeline? I may try the poker tables later and I hate to start a game with double gold eagles." He put two on the table. They were so new that the saw tooth edges were still sharp and clean. No one had taken a dozen of them, put them in a leather pouch and rattled them together to mint himself a half ounce of gold as the edges wore down.

Evangeline motioned to one of the house men watching play and he gave Spur ten ones and six fives.

"Now I'll be ready to play if I decide to," he said. Spur spun his hat on his finger, then eased it back on his head. Most of the men in the saloon wore their hats, cowboy fashion.

"Miss Evangeline. Would it be proper for me to ask you out to dinner tomorrow evening?"

"Might be, might not be. But it really doesn't matter. I don't go out much. Some of the snootier women in town think that I'm a fallen woman, a harbinger of doom, and the handmaiden of the devil. Although they don't really believe that I'm a maiden running an establishment such as I do."

Spur chuckled. "Sounds like you have a batch of God-fearing women in this town."

"Deed we do, Mr. McCoy, and two fire and brimstone preachers who do their best to scare each other and their respective congregations every Sunday morning and every Wednesday night at prayer meeting."

"Just so they won't be totally disappointed, I'll

play one hand of serial number poker with you on one of those fives you have. Deal?'' Evangeline smiled sweetly and dimpled both cheeks.

"Deal. And after that?''

"Next I have some business things to do in my office. I am running an establishment here. I have twelve employees and bills to pay and items to order. You know about a business.''

"Do you need any help?''

She started to smile, then her face shifted into a stern mask to cover her feelings.

"Mr. McCoy. I may run a saloon, but I am not a saloon girl. I don't go to bed with men for money. I don't invite men up to my bedroom on a whim. I was happily married for six years, and until I find a man I love and want to marry, I'll smile a lot and dress conservatively and make every effort to keep my knees pressed firmly together and my dress buttoned up to my chin.''

"You've said that before.''

"Twice a day for the past five years. More times on Saturdays.'' She looked up quickly. "Once in a great while I don't really mean it. Sometimes it gets lonely even in a crowded saloon.''

"Lonely I know something about,'' Spur said. He cleared his throat and tried to change the mood. "Now, you said something about a hand of five dollar bill serial poker. Do I get to pick one my six?''

Evangeline smiled, the somber mood broken. "Not a chance. Draw one out from the green side so you can't see the numbers. I'll do the same.'' She opened the drawer, leafed through a stack of bills until she came to the green side of some fives and pulled one out.

Spur picked one of his fives and turned it over to

the side where the serial number was. It read: 86617165. He had sixes over aces, a full house.

He looked at her and saw only a slightly serious poker face that told him nothing. "I'd really like to bet on the hand, but all we bet is the bill, right?"

"True," she said. "This would have been a great hand to play with. Would you believe I have a full house?"

Spur laughed. "That's what I've got. Can you top three sixes?"

"Can't top it but I can match it, and then throw in a pair of aces! No way you can beat that hand!"

Spur felt a shot of energy surge through his body. That was the exact serial number of the five dollar bill he held. That meant trouble. He tried to cover his concern.

"I'll be damned! That's the same number I have. Let's see."

They compared the bills on the table. They were exactly the same.

"How can that happen?" Evangeline asked.

"Doesn't happen often. Once in a while a printer forgets to move up the counter on the press. Whammo . . . two with the same number. Which means collectors will pay twice the face value for such a bill. I'll give you ten dollars for that fiver."

"Really? Best deal I've made all day. You'll probably sell it for ten times its face value, but I doubled my money." Spur gave her a ten dollar bill from his wallet and tucked the twin fives safely away.

Things were getting more interesting. Slocum must be dispensing medicine and counterfeits from the same location. Spur had asked for the five dollar bills because they were the denomination most widely counterfeited. Twenty dollar bills were too hard to pass. Lots of merchants hesitated to take them.

But a fiver was more standard. Lots of men worked for a week for five dollars. Counterfeiters found they could buy something for twenty cents and pass a fake five and get back four dollars and eighty cents in clear profit. A good buyer could pass a hundred fivers in a small town in a day and be on his horse heading for the next town away from the telegraph the next morning before anyone discovered the funny money.

Evangeline was laughing. "Hey, you were a million miles away there for a minute. You want to try one more game?"

Spur grinned but shook his head. "I think I better quit while I'm only out ten dollars. Truth to tell, I'm about asleep on my feet. That stage ride was wild, and sleep is one item I'm short on. If you don't mind, I better try to find my way back to the hotel."

"I could send a guide with you," she said.

He looked at her quickly and saw she was laughing at him. Suddenly she leaned in and kissed his cheek.

"There, that's to help scare away the lonelies. Stop by tomorrow and we'll talk again. I grew up just upstate from New York City a ways. We can do some old home talking." She stood and was gone before he could get to his feet.

Spur had started to rise, now he dropped back in the chair and checked the remaining five dollar bills he carried. Three more of them had the same serial number, counterfeit. The town must be flooded with them.

Tomorrow he would visit Doc Slocum about the

cough he had nights and mornings. Tomorrow he might also wrap up this case and get headed out for Denver.

He sipped the champagne in his glass. It wasn't his favorite drink. He picked up the bottle, stepped down from the platform and set the champagne on a table where four men were engaged in some serious beer drinking.

They looked up and then three of them grabbed the bottle at the same time.

At the bar, Spur caught the attention of the apron. "How much for the champagne?"

The bartender shook his head. "That's Miss Evangeline's table, sir. Never any charges there."

Spur nodded and walked out of the saloon and gaming house, wondering just now he could trip up Doc George Slocum into giving away where his printing press was. That was vital, he had to have the press and the plates for a conviction.

Outside, Spur turned down Main Street, walked two blocks to where the stores thinned out an occasional house showed. The third one on the left was Doc Slocum's office. The lower floors were dark, but there were lights on in the top floor. Office? Home?

Maybe an office, home and printing plant. Spur hoped so. He had no desire to spend any more time in this little town than he needed to.

Spur headed back for his hotel room. He guessed the hot-blooded maid would be through with her duties for the day. A grin spread across his face. She had been delightful, such a healthy young thing and so eager. If he stayed in town more than three or four days, he made a small bet with himself that she would be back to see him.

He thought of the teenager, the redheaded boy

who thought Spur was a lawman. The kid was closer to being right than Spur wanted him to know. Spur remembered his own youth. Growing up was harder than adults remembered.

Especially it would be tough for Willard, moving here from Chicago, leaving all his friends, and coming into a rougher, more action oriented society. Spur wished Willard all the good fortune he could get.

Willard sat in his room at the small desk and finished the last chapter of the Western dime novel. Big John had been beaten in a shootout and the ranch was saved for the widow Beluchi. She asked Lew Hardison in for supper. Lew had killed Big John and saved the ranch for her. Willard knew that Lew was not going to be out on the trail that night. It was all very straightlaced in the book, but Willard knew what would happen.

"Blow out that lamp, Willard!" a shrill voice came up the stairs. "Past your bedtime."

"Yes, Aunt Zelda," Willard said. His mother had been dead almost five years. He missed her. She hadn't been as cranky and mean as Aunt Zelda. She acted like she wished he had never come. Willard never mentioned the twenty dollars a month his aunt and uncle got from his estate, but he wondered what they did with it. Hardly any of it was spent on him.

He slid onto the bed. He wouldn't need covers for some time yet. The afternoon heat was still in the attic and seeping down into his room.

Willard kicked out of the bottom half of his long johns and lay there naked. For just a moment his imagination flashed back to the end of the dime novel story. He wondered what that cowboy was going to do with the widow. He had ideas. He'd heard about it, about a man and a woman doing it.

His hand brushed his crotch.

Oh, yes! Willard had an instant erection, hot blood pounding and pounding. That made him remember Chicago. One week he had walked around school all day with a hard-on. It just wouldn't go away.

That was the week Martha had kissed him behind the band shell in the park. She had kissed him and then let him touch her breasts through her dress.

But just for a moment. Then she ran back with the three girls she was with and wouldn't even look at him. He had made a mess in his pants right there before he could move.

It had felt so good!

Willard's hand closed around his hard pole and he knew it would feel good again.

But he shouldn't do it.

Why not? Who said? He'd seen guys have a contest once and neither of them grew hair on the palm of his hand. That wasn't true.

He stroked it once, then again. He really shouldn't. He remembered Martha and how soft she had been. Were all girls tits that soft? Willard let his imagination take over then. Martha was there and they kissed again, then she let him touch her and he pulled her dress open and pushed his hands inside.

Her breasts were so warm! So soft and warm. She had shivered and said she liked the way he felt of her. She put her hand down lower and pressed it against his bulge. Then she opened his pants and tried to pull him out.

Willard helped. Then her breasts were bare and

she told him to kiss them. He did and his hips bucked and she shivered and shook and he pushed her down, his hips pounding against hers even though she still had her dress on.

Willard heard his aunt and uncle walk by in the hall and his hips stilled. When they were in their bedroom he turned over and rammed his erection against the sheet. He was with Martha again and she was helping him and spreading her legs, and then . . . then . . .

He didn't have to imagine any more. His hips bucked spasmodically six, seven, eight times and he shot his cream all over the sheet.

Willard panted and gasped for breath. Someday he wouldn't have to imagine what it was like. He would have a girl and they would do it and it would be wonderful!

He found an old handkerchief and wiped up the sticky goo from the blanket and threw the handkerchief in the back of the closet.

Then he lay on his bed thinking about Martha, and about the lawman he had met today. He was positive that Mr. McCoy was a lawman. But he shivered when he remembered the two desperados who had sneaked into town. They were going to rob the bank, he was sure of it!

Tomorrow he would get up his courage to go tell the sheriff. He thought about that for a minute. No, the sheriff wouldn't believe him. He'd see Mr. McCoy. Willard was sure that Mr. McCoy would be interested in bank robbers.

Every lawman was duty bound to protect the banks and to stop any bank robbers they saw.

Willard nodded and wavered toward sleep. He thought of Martha, and for just a moment she was naked. Standing in front of him without a thing on! Then she smiled and faded away, and Willard Kleaner slept.

5

Spur McCoy slept in the next morning. He woke at his usual 5:30, turned over and went back to sleep. He was up at eight o'clock, dressed, shaved, had a leisurely breakfast at a small cafe and arrived at Doc Slocum's office promptly at nine.

He worked up a small cough and would keep clearing his throat. There was no one else in the doctor's office when he walked in and a small bell rang over the door.

A moment later a man about five-six came through the connecting door. He wore a white shirt and red suspenders. Dr. Slocum was slightly on the chubby side, with pink cheeks and alert brown eyes. He had a full head of dark hair.

Spur heard chairs scraping and small feet running upstairs. So Slocum had become a family man.

"Are you Doc Slocum?" Spur asked.

"Guess you're out of luck, that's me. You look healthy enough."

"Wish I was, Doc. Got this cough that's been hanging on. You help me lick it, Doc?"

The brown eyes sparkled. "Toughest medical problem I had all day. I got a jug of cherry cough syrup back here that'll knock out any cough. Don't say for sure, but I'd guess it's got some laudanum in it. I used some once and for a couple of hours I didn't *care* if I had a cough or not!"

Spur coughed again and Slocum waved and went into the back room. Spur looked on the office walls, but saw no framed medical diplomas.

Lots of the far West doctors didn't have complete medical training. The pioneers in the West took what doctoring they could get and were glad for it.

The doctor came through the door carrying a small bottle that had a white label.

"Two teaspoons full of this as needed," Doctor Slocum said. "Any other problems?"

"Just a small brown haired lady that I'm going to have to handle myself Doc. How much do I owe you?"

"Fifty cents'll be fine. I don't get a lot of cash money in payment these days. Lot of chickens and loaves of bread and a quart of milk a day. That comes in handy. You be from the east, Boston, I'd say by the twang."

"Went to school a while there," Spur said. "Thought I'd lost it. You sound more from Virginia or maybe Washington, D.C."

Slocum looked up at Spur but saw that the big man was only making conversation.

Spur handed the doctor one of the fake five dollars bills. The medic stared at it and shook his head.

"Sorry, don't have change enough. Just owe me like everybody else in town does."

Spur put the fiver back in his wallet and fumbled in his pocket until he found two 1875 minted twenty cent pieces and a dime. He handed them to the doctor.

"Think these new twenty cent pieces will last?" Spur asked. "I keep getting them mixed up with the quarters."

"Won't last. A damn nuisance. Won't last more than two or three years. Then the collectors can make money on them. My advice, keep all you can find and give them to your grandchildren. Be able to put themselves through school with them."

Spur tossed the bottle of cough syrup in the air and caught it. "Thanks, Doc. I just got into town. You know of any businesses for sale? I'm looking for something."

"Always one or two available. Just so you aren't another doctor."

"Not a chance. Thanks, Doc." Spur went out the front door and walked quickly down the street. Slocum had not taken the five dollar bill. Had he guessed it was fake, or was he simply out of change? He did know about coins, but everybody had something to say about the new twenty cent piece.

Spur hesitated about taking the local sheriff into his confidence about the fake money. He didn't want to start a panic. The quieter this could be kept the better. If he could scoop up Slocum, his plates and press in one bunch, then he would go to the banker and they could begin gathering up the bad bills without anyone the wiser.

To lay a foundation for that move, Spur walked toward the bank. It was nearly ready to open. He toured two more stores and talked to their owners. Neither wanted to sell. They knew about him though, and were pleased that he had asked them. Always nice to be asked to dance even though you have a broken leg.

At the bank he asked to see the manager. The man turned out to be Barton Concord. He was a tall man, and slender, with a thin face, protruding eyebrows and deep set eyes that reminded Spur of Abe Lincoln. Concord wore a banker black three piece suit with a stiff collar and carefully tied cravat.

He was cautious, friendly, reserved. He seemed to be the form they used to turn out bankers these days.

"Mr. Concord. My name is Spur McCoy and I'm looking for a business property here in town, as I'm sure you have heard by now."

Concord smiled. It was not a banker's smile. "Yes, Mr. McCoy, news travels fast in a small town. Everyone knows by now. By the time Hans Walker gets his paper out you'll be old news."

"That's one of the reasons I want to settle in a small town. Everyone knows everyone else." Spur chuckled. "Of course that means you have to be a bit careful with your public conduct." Both men laughed.

"Well, Mr. Concord. Being a merchant I handle a lot of paper money, and I found a bill in my change that didn't look exactly right. Would you take a look at it for me?"

Spur handed the banker one of the counterfeit fivers and sat back. Concord turned it over, rubbed it between his fingers and crumpled it up. When he straightened it out on his desk top he nodded, then handed it back to Spur.

"Far as I can see it's a one hundred percent guaranteed U.S. banknote. Looks genuine to me. Course

I have been fooled once or twice, but I'm pretty good at bills."

"Good. That was my one concern. I certainly wouldn't want to start a business in a town where there was bad currency. No, no I won't start any rumors. That's why I came to see you first. It has been a year or so since I had my own store, so my fingers have lost the touch. I used to be able to tell by the quality of the paper when I got a bad bill. Didn't happen often, of course."

"Mr. McCoy, when you locate the right business and make a purchase, I hope you'll do your banking here with us. We're not the oldest bank in the county, but we think the most friendly. We could even arrange some kind of a loan or a mortgage on property, that sort of thing to get you started."

"Thanks, but I have more than adequate financing. Well, thanks, Mr. Concord. I have some more ground work to do. You'll be hearing from me in due course."

They shook hands and Spur left the solid brick building. He was puzzled. On close comparison with a genuine bank note there was no doubt that the bill was a counterfeit, even without the proof of the serial numbers.

Concord must not know his business. Of course he didn't handle the actual bills much on a day to day basis from the looks of the bank. He had three tellers and a bookkeeper. Adequate. He'd put Bart Concord in the uncertain file for now.

Spur stopped at two more stores, talked to the owners, hinted at what he might offer for one store and was turned down. He had to keep his offers low enough to discourage a sale.

Where would Slocum do his printing? Newspaper.

COLORADO CUTIE

Every newspaper in the west had a small job press or two for stationery and business forms. Spur found the newspaper office where the *Johnson County Voice* was created once a week.

As soon as he opened the door, a familiar and slightly nostagic odor assaulted him. It was a combination of the smell of newsprint and all kinds of paper goods, mixed with the slightly acrid odor of printer's ink and the cleaning fluids they used on the presses. Every newspaper in the country had that same smell.

There was a chest high counter across the front of the office. Behind it a man sat at a desk stacked with papers and galley proofs. Beside him at a second desk a woman looked up, rose and came to the counter.

"Good morning. You must be Spur McCoy, the gentleman in town looking for a business to buy. How about a newspaper? I've been trying to get Hans out of here for three years now."

"This establishment is not for sale," the man at the desk said without turning around. His pencil made a correction on a galley proof and he pushed it over to the next desk the woman had just left.

She smiled at Spur. He smiled back. She was attractive, in her late twenties and not yet ground down by hard work.

"Now that we have that out of the way, what can we do for you, Mr. McCoy?"

"I find I need some cards, twenty-five, maybe fifty, with my hotel address on them. You do commercial printing?"

The man stood quickly and turned.

"Damn right! That's how we stay alive in this god-forsaken hole. Certainly not be selling advertising in the *Voice.*" He pulled out a type sample book and began showing Spur the typefaces.

"Mr. Walker I would guess," Spur said.

The man grunted, held out his hand. "Yes, and you're McCoy. We can give you fifty cards by four o'clock this afternoon. Just pick out the type style you like."

"Mr. Walker, you're far more skilled at those matters than I am. Make me a card you'd be proud to give out yourself. I'll put down my name, the Aspen Hotel and say, businessman. That will do it."

Hans wrote down what Spur told him, then he took another sheet of newsprint. "You looking for any particular type of business, Mr. McCoy?"

"No, but in the retail field I think."

"Been looking long, in other towns as well?"

"Yes, I'm working west. Denver will be my next stop I think. But I'd rather be out here."

The interview went on for another five minutes. Spur said nothing about his real purpose for being in town. He asked how much the printing would be and the man gave him a price without any figuring.

"Three dollars."

Spur handed him one of the counterfeit bills and Walker took it without hesitation. He didn't even examine it as he put it in a small money box under the counter and handed Spur two singles.

"Thank you, I'll be back at four." Spur tipped his hat to the woman and walked out. He had been able to see in the back room of the newspaper plant. It had a sheet fed press as well as two smaller job presses, platen type. Either one was good enough to print the currency. Another spot to watch.

Spur moved slowly down the street to the Moon's General Store where he spotted four captain's chairs next to the outside wall. Two men sat in them. They were old men watching the world sail by now instead of doing the rowing.

Spur eased into one of the vacant chairs and tipped it back against the building. The sun came down warm on his face. He slid his hat down over his eyes so it shaded them, but left him a small area of vision.

For the next hour he sat there, watching Main Street, checking every now and then the front door of Dr. George Slocum. He had seen three women go in, and one man, then two kids and their mother. The doctor did not go out for a noon time dinner. He probably ate upstairs with his family when the office emptied.

Spur wasn't sure if he were really expecting the doctor to leave in the middle of the day, or if he just liked sitting there in the sun.

This was the craziest assignment he'd ever had. His orders were to go get a guy who might not be the man the Service was hunting after all. Bring him back to Denver, but first be sure he was the right man.

It certainly didn't make it any easier. In five minutes he was going to get up and take the next step in his investigation, whatever that was. Maybe Evangeline. She probably knew a little about almost everyone in town, and the habits of some of the men better than most. Yes, in just five minutes he would have another talk with Evangeline.

Willard Kleaner walked down Third Street toward Main. He looked again. Nope, no hair grew in the palms of his hands. He thought about the night before and grinned. Martha had looked so great all naked that way, but the picture had faded out too quickly.

Just thinking about the vision started action at his crotch and he deliberately moved his mind to something else. The robbers! He had decided last night that he was going to tell Mr. McCoy about them. How did he find the lawman?

He was half way to Main when he saw a lone rider coming in from the Denver trail. The man was slouching in the saddle, a sure sign that he had been on a long ride. He had a dirty bandage around his left arm, and as he came closer, Willard could see a patch over one eye held in place by a black band around his cheek and over his forehead.

Willard turned up an alley and crept back to watch the man pass. The desperado had hired killer written all over him. On his right thigh a hogleg was tied low, the way killers did it. A rifle rested in the saddle boot. No bedroll, no grub sack. The man was traveling light and fast, the way Kirk Dawson did in *Killer on the Run.*

The man was a vicious desperado alright! Willard followed him down the street well back, and when he turned right on Main, Willard was sure about him. That was where most of the saloons were. The first thing a killer did when he was running from a dastardly deed was to get drunk.

Willard came around the small saloon at the juncture of Main and Third, just in time to see the killer get off his horse and limp heavily as he went into the Three Aces Saloon. A morning drinker, a limp from long days in the saddle, and a tied down gun. Not even counting the eye patch the man had labeled himself a desperate killer of the worst kind.

Willard stood there pondering his moves. He could go directly to the sheriff. But that might not work. He could hire one of the ten year old's hanging around Main Street to take a note to the sheriff.

Or he could try to find Spur McCoy. Willard decided on the latter plan and walked down Main Street toward the hotel. He had five minutes before he had to be to work at the Aspen. This was more important anyway. A killer in town should not be tolerated. He had to be routed or captured quickly before his evil ways would spread.

Willard stopped as he passed the hardware. There in front of the General Store sat Spur McCoy. Willard recognized him by the string of silver pesos serving as a headband around his hat.

Now all he had to do was go up and talk. Willard suddenly felt that his hands had no connection whatsoever with the rest of his body. He didn't know where to put them. They hung like dead appendages on the end of his long arms.

For a moment he wasn't sure if he could walk. Would he have to think of every motion, tell his legs how to walk?

Willard turned and stared into the hardware. Maybe he shouldn't bother the lawman. He must be in town on a highly secret and important case. The killer might be running away from a murder like the guy in the novel was. Of course the killer in the story really didn't do it, he had been framed.

But this guy, with the wounded arm, the limp and the patch over one eye . . . there was no doubt about him being a killer.

Willard set his jaw firmly. Mr. McCoy said that in the West fifteen and a half was almost a man. He had *to act like a man!* He took the first step and then the next, gaining confidence with each one as he marched straight for Spur McCoy sitting leaned back against the General Store.

6

Willard Kleaner stopped abruptly in front of Spur
McCoy's chair where he had tipped it back in front
of Moon's General Store. Willard was shaking now,
he was on the delicate point of turning to run when
Spur pushed his hat back on his head and grinned.

"Willard, good morning. You look all fired up and
full of purpose this morning. What's on your mind?"

"There . . . there was a man . . ." He tried to go on,
couldn't and turned.

"Willard, just relax and take a deep breath or
two," Spur said standing beside the boy. "Easy,
relax a minute. You have nothing to be worried
about. Now where did you see this man?"

Willard wiped sweat off his forehead. His hand
still shook. He pushed both hands into his pockets.

"The man was on Third, coming into town."

"Yes. Why did you notice him, Willard?"

"He looked sneaky, and mean. He had a rifle and a
pistol tied low on his thigh and . . . and he had a

56

black patch over one eye. I'm sure he's a killer running away from some foul murder!" At last he got warmed up and had raced through the last sentence.

"This man rode into town?"

"Sure did. Went into the Three Aces Saloon. He even had a bloody bandage on his left arm. All bloody!"

"You think I should go down and see if he's an outlaw?" Spur asked.

Willard nodded. "Yes."

"Fine, Willard. I'll drop down that way. Are you going to be late getting to your job?"

Willard lifted his brows, turned and ran toward the Aspen Hotel. Spur adjusted his hat, put it back on his head exactly right, and walked toward the sign of the saloon Willard had mentioned.

For an Eastern boy, Willard had a good eye for detail. Inside the Three Aces Saloon, Spur bought a cold beer and saw the man Willard had mentioned. He was at the end of the bar talking with a man wearing a dark gray town suit and string tie over a white shirt.

When the men parted a little, Spur saw a sheriff's star on the town man. Spur motioned to the barkeep.

"Who's the Jasper talking to the sheriff?"

The bar man shrugged, then laughed. "Hell, that's the sheriff's top deputy without his badge. Looks like he was in a real showdown with somebody. I better give him a free beer. You want another one?"

Spur declined, finished the one he had and went out to the boardwalk.

Willard stood near the front steps to the Aspen

Hotel as Spur came striding up.

"The joke is on us," Spur said.

Willard looked up, anxious.

"Turns out the man you saw coming into town was a lawman himself, just back from a tough fight with a bunch of outlaws. He's one of the sheriff's deputies."

"Oh." Willard said. "Guess I was wrong. Thanks . . . Mr. McCoy. I'll be more careful next time."

"Willard, nothing hurt. You see somebody you think might be doing wrong, it's your duty to report it to the sheriff, or to me if I'm around. Now, you best be getting yourself inside before your uncle sends the sheriff out looking for you!"

Willard grinned. "Yeah. I guess so. Thanks . . . Mr. McCoy." He ran up the steps.

Spur wished his problem could be solved so simply. He remembered where he was going when he first saw Willard. His supply of .45 rounds was getting low, he needed some more. Spur walked across the street and down to the Johnson Mercantile. It was one of the smaller stores, but Spur figured they would have pistol rounds.

Windows on the boardwalk showed off displays of household items, as well as bolts of cloth and sheves of hand tools. Inside it was cool and dim. He paused a moment to adjust his eyes, then saw a well arranged display of counters and islands filled with merchandise. It reminded him of some of his father's stores in New York.

"Yes, may I help you?" a strong, woman's voice sounded from near the back of the store. Spur moved that way and soon saw a tall, slender woman standing behind a small counter.

"Morning, ma'am. I'm looking for some .45 rounds, Remingtons if you have them."

"Yes, we have them, over here."

Now he could see her better. She had long black hair that flowed over her shoulders and down her back. It framed a thin face with high cheek bones and from a quick look, he thought green eyes. She walked like a dancer going across a stage.

A smile flashed across her round, pert face.

"Hear you're in town to buy out a business. This one is for sale."

"Interesting," he said following her to a case near the far wall where an assortment of handguns were displayed and behind them rifles and shotguns in a wall rack. "How much are you asking for the business and the stock?"

"I own the building, too. I need seven thousand five hundred for the whole thing." She stopped and put one hand on her hip in a defiant pose, as if she were challenging him to try to bluff her down.

"Interesting. I'm not sure what I want to buy yet. I'll take two boxes of the .45's, please."

She pushed the rounds across the counter to him, took his money and gave him change. Then her whole attitude seemed to change. Her smile was warmer, her arms were not defiantly posed. He thought she held herself so her breasts pressed tighter against her dress.

"Could I show you around? We have a good sized storage room in back for downstock, and there's a rear delivery door on the alley. Yes! Let me lock the front door and I'll give you a guided tour. I haven't thought too much about selling but I know I should."

She walked quickly to the front, snapped a night lock and put a sign up that said "Closed, Be Back Soon."

Back at the counter she waved at the stock. "I

have a good general merchandise variety. I try to keep up on the catalogs and what people like. Here we have items for the house and kitchen and even the yard and workshop. We have a good variety of tools as well."

She waved at islands on either side of the main aisle.

"Now, Mr. McCoy, if you'll step this way to our storage room, I'll show you what else we have. I'm sorry, that 'we' is not right. I said that for so long it's hard to break the habit. You see, my father built the store, ran it for almost twenty years. I can't remember him not being here when I was a little girl.

"The big pox epidemic five years ago just rose up and hit our town hard. We had eight people die, all within a week of each other. Daddy just couldn't fight it off. Not even Doc Slocum could save him, but he tried hard.

"Oh, excuse me. My name is Priscilla Davis. Everyone in town knows who you are. We don't have a lot of strangers in Johnson Corners."

"Thank you, Miss Davis, but I really have to be looking at some more stores."

"You've hardly seen anything here yet. I insist." She caught his arm and pulled tightly against him. He was strongly aware of her breasts pressed against his arm.

"Now, behind the counter is the storage and back stock area." She led him through an opening in the wall into the next room. It had stacks of unopened boxes. Some rolls of barbed wire and some heavier hardware items such as pipe and roofing and kegs of nails.

She kept his arm tightly imprisoned by her hand

and her breast. He could feel the heat of it through her dress. The blue gingham was prim and proper, buttoned to the chin with long sleeves and ruffles at her wrists. The dress swept the floor as she walked showing not even a hint of ankle.

"My father was an excellent merchant. He taught me how to stock and how to display the goods. He told me over and over again that you can't sell a washtub without showing washtubs."

She stopped and watched him a moment. "Mr. McCoy, you look like an intelligent, kind, understanding man. I have a problem that I think you can help me with, if you only will."

Spur grinned. "I often help damsels in distress, Miss Davis."

"Good." She smiled then a frown stained her face. "This is what my mother would call a highly personal problem. It embarrasses me to mention it, but I have to grab the opportunity while I can."

They went around a stack of boxes and found a walled off section of the storeroom.

"Oh, I built a small apartment back here to help save money. I don't need much room. Could I make you a cup of tea?"

Spur frowned for a moment, then shrugged. "I'm never likely to turn down tea with an attractive lady."

Priscilla smiled. "You've very kind. Come in, it isn't much but it's all I need."

The small room held a bed, a tiny wood stove with a chimney, a wash stand and a dresser. The single bed was covered with a beautiful spread and three pink pillows. There was only one chair.

"Sit down while I light the fire and put on the teapot. It won't take but a minute."

He chose the chair and when she had the fire lit, she moved to the bed and sat down.

For a moment she looked straight at him, and Spur was struck by the honesty in her eyes, in her whole manner.

"Mr. McCoy. I told you I have this small problem. You see, there's a wonderful man in town who has asked me to marry him. I said of course, but he put one condition on it. This gentleman is . . . I don't know the word, but he is unable to perform sexually."

She turned away and he saw a blush on her neck and cheek. "This is difficult for me, and I ask your patience." A minute later she looked back at Spur. The fire crackled in the stove.

"He was open and frank with me. A war wound, he said. His heart's desire is to have children, at least to let the community think that he has children."

Priscilla took a deep breath, and then rushed ahead. "He said the only way he can marry me is if I will get pregnant first!" She hurried on. "Yes, I know, shocking. But when you think of it, practical. How else could we have a family? I told him I would try. But in a small town, talk gets around. The whole idea is to let the town think the child is Milton's."

To cover her embarrassment she went to the stove and took off the boiling pot and poured tea. Then she turned. She had unbuttoned half of the fasteners of her blouse and now walked toward him slowly. She undid more buttons.

"Mr. McCoy, I would be so unendingly grateful to you if you could try to . . . you know . . . to make me pregnant. I told you this was a highly personal and a delicate problem."

She had the buttons open to her waist. Quickly she shrugged out of the top of the dress letting it fall, then unhooked a binder that covered her breasts and slowly let it slide down. Her twin mounds of flesh were revealed slowly, first the rounded swell, then the breasts and at last the small nipples of pink, set in large areolas of darker pink.

Spur shifted in the chair. She stood directly in front of him, her bared breasts at eye level.

"Miss Davis, I don't see how . . ."

She moved forward, caught the back of his head and brought his mouth slowly toward her right breast.

"You are an attractive woman, Miss Davis. Beautiful. But I don't see how . . ."

Then her nipple brushed his lips and with a small moan he opened his mouth and accepted her offering. He licked her breast, chewed on it, nibbled at her nipple until she began to writhe in delight.

She moved so he could minister to her left breast, and then she sat down on the bed and pulled him over beside her. She flipped up the skirt of her dress and lifted it over her head. She wore the kind of underwear that fit tightly down to the knee.

At once she began taking off Spur's clothes. He hesitated, caught her hands and watched her. But she pulled his hands to her breasts and he laughed softly.

"All right, all right. I'll help you with your small problem. With a lady as beautiful as you, I wouldn't think you would have any trouble at all."

"Getting pregnant? Oh, but I don't want to let just any man father my first child. He must be tall and strong and handsome like you." She pulled open his belt and then his town pants and pushed them down.

For a moment she worked at his underwear, then she yelped in joy as his stiff penis popped out slanting up at a forty-five degree angle, hard and ready to perform.

Without a moment's hesitation, Priscilla bent and kissed his throbbing tool.

"Oh, yes, just perfect! So big and long. He'll plant your seed deep inside me so they can make me pregnant this very morning!"

Eagerly she slipped out of the tight, white cotton drawers, and squirmed naked on the bed, her black pubic triangle quivering.

"Hurry, hurry!" she said.

Spur pulled off his boots, then the rest of his clothes and lay down beside her.

"Quickly, quickly! I don't want to lose another minute. Push it inside me right now. I want to get pregnant this very moment!"

She was soft and moist and open. Her legs had spread and knees lifted and Priscilla watched him with glistening, bright eyes.

"Yes, Spur McCoy! Oh, yes, push it in me hard and fast. I want it right now. All of it! All of you!"

Hell, I'm only human, Spur thought as he went between her legs and eased forward. She accepted him with a squeal. Her hips shot up to meet him and she lunged and moaned with each thrust.

"Yes, yes! Harder, faster! Plant those seeds of yours deep! I want to be pregnant in two minutes!"

Spur grinned. He could never remember being in quite this situation before. Below him, Priscilla became totally erotic, reacting to every movement with a shout or squeal or moan of satisfaction and fulfillment.

She slammed through two climaxes so close

together that they blended into one and all the time she encouraged Spur to reach his own satisfaction.

By that time Spur was so worked up he knew it wouldn't take long, and he panted and then gasped and grunted as he felt the floodgates opening and he pounded fast and furious into her eager body. She lifted her legs over his back and locked them together, accepting his thrusts with a shout of joy each time.

"I know this is the one!" she called. "No, this time, this is the time I get pregnant!"

When Spur fell on top of her with a long wheezing sigh, and began gasping for breath, she smiled and locked her arms around his back.

"Wonderful!" she whispered in his ear. "Now, twice more today, just to be sure."

Spur heard her in the fuzzy haze of his mini death, and shook his head. "I have business to take care of, Priscilla."

"Not as important as this," she said. "Hush now and rest up, I need you again, soon."

Fifteen minutes later, Spur got up and dressed, over her protests.

"I have to make sure. Once is fine, but three times is best. That's what all my lady friends tell me."

"Priscilla, I told you I have important business. The first time is always the most potent. That's the best I can do. Now you better open the store, don't you think?"

"This way?" She stood up and twirled around. She was still naked. Her breasts bounced delightfully. Spur almost weakened.

"However you think you can make the most sales, Priscilla," he said. "I'll let myself out the back way."

"No! You can't go!" She jumped in front of the

door. Spur picked her up by her waist and moved her out of the way.

"Good luck on your quest, Priscilla," Spur said, then he went out the door, and slipped through the door on the alley and walked around to Main Street. He wanted to watch the newspaper office. As far as he knew that was the only printing press in town.

7

For the rest of the day, Spur watched the newspaper office and printing plant. He lifted a cold beer in a saloon where he could look out the window at the place. Later he walked around to the alley and peered at the rear door. Nothing happened. Nobody went in or out. The press was not working. The newspaper would be out Thursday morning.

By mid afternoon he gave up and began talking in saloons about Doc Slocum. He found out little about the man's background. Almost nobody knew much about him. A few men said he was in town when they arrived. One barkeep said he heard the doc came from back East somewhere.

There was agreement about one thing. Doc Slocum was the only doctor in town, and they would fight to keep him from leaving. They might even consider paying what they owed him to keep him in Johnson Corners.

Spur stopped by at the barber shop, sat in the

chairs until it was his turn and got his neck trimmed and his thick reddish brown hair thinned out a little. The moustache clip was free.

"Hear we got a good doctor in town," Spur ventured.

Slim of Slim's Barbershop snapped the long barber scissors twice near Spur's ear and stared at him.

"Only damn one we've got. Don't matter none how good he is. He's here and he's ours. Belongs to the town you might say. So good don't matter."

"About the size of it," Spur agreed. "Know where he came from? Seems like most folks here come from somewhere else."

"Don't know, don't care." Slim snipped some more. "Just so he stays here. Got my young'un over a bout of near pneumonia last winter. Doc's an all right guy in my book."

By the time the haircut was over, Spur knew little more about Doc Slocum.

He had missed lunch, so he got a sandwich at a small cafe. He ordered thin sliced roast beef with lots of lettuce and a big dill pickle. The waitress was tired before she got to work. She might also own the small eatery, he couldn't tell. She made the sandwich from homemade bread, slicing the roast beef with a wicked looking, twelve-inch blade.

She reacted to his question about Doc quickly.

"Nope, don't know where he comes from. We got a habit in this town of not prying too much about folks. Don't care where they been. Just care how they act while they here. Might be a good idea for you to do the same. You're a stranger in town. Everybody knows that. They say you're looking to buy a business. That true?"

"Yes, that was my intention. But I want to be sure the town has the basics like a doctor, a good sheriff, law and order, and some good spots to eat."

"We got them," she said with a grin. "Especially the eats, like here. You ever have a better roast beef sandwich?"

"Matter of fact, I can't remember one," Spur said. They chatted about the weather and the town until Spur had finished his sandwich. He paid for it and left feeling vaguely impatient. He wasn't getting anywhere with his investigation. How could he be sure Doc Slocum was the man Washington wanted?

How could he be sure that the Doc was spreading the fake five dollar bills around? He needed some evidence, but that seemed hard to find. No wonder somebody had put a proviso on his orders.

Poker! A good tough game of poker always cleared his mind. Gave him a new perspective on a problem. He walked down the street to the Evangeline and found a seat on a poker table. He bought in with a double eagle, and a half hour later he had about seventy-five dollars worth of chips in front of him.

A new player slid into a chair across from him.

Evangeline herself.

He started to get up, but the other three men in the game did not.

She smiled and motioned for him to sit down. It was his deal.

"Five card stud, two cards down, five dollars ante," he said.

Evangeline nodded and put a five dollar chip into the pot from her stack on the table.

"Table stakes, no new money," Spur said. He shuffled the cards, placed the deck flat on the table top and carefully passed out two down cards to each player. There was twenty-five dollars in the pot—a cowboy's wages for a month.

He slid the next card off the top of the deck and placed it face up to the first man, and did so for each player. Evangeline had an ace of hearts, and high. She bet two dollars. Spur had a King showing. He looked at his hole cards, A King and an Ace. Cut down the odds of her having a pair. He raised it five dollars and everyone stayed in.

On the second round he called them as he played the cards face up around the circle.

"A four and a seven. A pair of sixes, Queen and a King possible straight." Evangeline had an Ace and a seven. His own King caught a ten, no help.

"Pair of sixes bets," Spur said.

"Two dollars," the cowboy said.

Everyone stayed in, nobody raised.

Spur dealt the third card face up and called the round.

"Four, seven and a six. Possible straight, ruins the man's three sixes." The second player caught a Queen. "Pair of sixes and a Queen. No help there." The third man got his Jack. "Jack, Queen and King. Possible straight. Now for the lady." He dealt out an Ace. "Pair of Aces for the business woman." he slid his card off and turned it up. "A King, pair of Kings. Pair of Aces high bets."

Evangeline looked at the cards, stared at the possible straight and without changing her expression pushed out two ten dollar chips. Spur was next to her, he met the bet and added a fiver.

"Twenty-five to you, sir," Spur said. The 4-7-6 hand man folded. The pair of sixes and Queen studied his hand, then shook his head and threw his cards face down on the chips.

The last man snorted and threw in his hand. Evangeline looked at Spur. "Let's see your five, and add another twenty. How good a gambler are you, McCoy?"

Spur stared at the pair of Aces. Not good odds that she could have three Aces with a third one showing. Two sixes were up so she could not get a full house. Two pair? Possible but he had his three Kings, even with one King showing.

Spur pushed in the twenty, he had four dollars left. "And raise you four, my limit."

Evangeline frowned slightly as she looked at his cards, then added four one dollar chips to the pot.

"Call," she said softly.

Spur turned over his third King. "Three wise men from afar," he said.

Evangeline scooped up her cards and threw them face down on the pot. "Beats me," she said.

Spur pulled in the pot, over a hundred and sixty-five dollars.

The deal went around and Spur lost twenty dollars on the next two bad hands. On the third one he lost fifty on a pair of Aces, but when Evangeline dealt he had two Queens on a hand of five card draw. He opened for ten dollars on the Jacks or better rule and threw away three cards. Everyone knew he had a pair. He drew the first three cards and sat back not looking at them. Two of the men looked at their cards and threw them in. Evidently they were beaten by his pair.

The third man frowned down a smile and held. Evangeline took two cards. Was she filling or bluffing?

Spur looked at his cards close to his chest, edging one into view at a time. Besides the pair of Queens, he had a seven, then came a three. Not much help.

The last card was another seven. Two pair.

A weak hand to be betting on. He checked the bet and the man across looked up quickly and bet ten dollars. Evangeline met it and raised him ten.

Twenty to Spur. He took a slow breath folded his cards and laid them face down in front of him. Then he pushed two tens into the pot.

The man across from Spur added a ten.

"Call," he said.

Evangeline laid down three fours. "Is that enough?" she asked. The men dropped their cards face down and she pulled in the pot.

Two hours later, Spur was down to twenty-five dollars. He was five dollars ahead.

"I'm out," Spur said standing up. It was getting toward five o'clock and he was no farther along with his case—either of them. Evangeline stood as well. She walked away and he followed her to the bar.

Spur stopped beside her. "Could I take the big winner out to dinner?" he asked.

She smiled. "Best place in town?" she asked.

He nodded.

"I'll be ready in ten minutes. Don't get lost."

She hurried toward the back stairs.

A half hour later Spur and Evangeline settled down at a table at a small eatery just off Main Street. It featured "Authentic New Orleans Ribs," and was run by a black husband and wife team.

"You didn't blink when I suggested ribs," Evangeline said. "Which means you've had them down south somewhere."

"New Orleans," Spur said, slurring the words together with the accent of the "or" the way the natives say it.

"You do get around. I still wonder why you're

here. You don't seem to be buying a business very fast."

"I'm a cautious man."

"Not the way you play poker you aren't."

"Where I really am conservative is in my choice of women."

She laughed. "Now I know you're bluffing me. I'd raise right now on a pair of Jacks."

"I opened with Jacks but I have an Ace high," he said.

She shook her head. "Not good enough, cowboy. I've got an Ace-King high."

He grinned and their salads came, huge helpings of tossed greenery with strips of carrots and wedges of tomatoes and some potent dressing.

They worked on the salad silently for a few minutes.

"Are you going to stay here in Johnson Corners forever?" he asked.

"Probably. I've got some roots down."

"But no family."

"I'm an only child. Both my parents are dead. I've never been close to any of the rest of my family tree. Two whole limbs have refused to talk to me since I began running the saloon, so I'm not missing much."

"I was thinking about a family of your own, establishing the Evangeline dynasty, and a string of gaming houses across the west, maybe a partnership with the Overland Stage Lines."

She laughed and bit a carrot stick in half.

"No such ambitions. Running one gaming house takes all of my time."

"Delegate responsibility."

"In a saloon that's a license to steal. Have you

ever seen an honest barkeep? There's no way to know how many drinks they pour. How do you keep track?"

"True. I knew a saloon owner in Kansas once. When he tended bar he even stole from himself!"

Their ribs came then, a huge platter filled with pork ribs and lathered with a barbecue sauce that stood up and said hello half way to your mouth.

The light skinned black woman brought the ribs and then tied big white bibs around their necks and gave them two linen napkins each.

"Just so you can enjoy your ribs," she said with a smile that showed gleaming white teeth. "Y'all enjoy your dinner now, y'hear?"

They were black-eyed peas and turnip greens and slabs of thick white bread, fresh salted butter and a covered pot of blackberry jam. The coffee came steaming hot in the cup with a heavy crockery pitcher full on the side.

"Now these are ribs!" Spur said after the first bite. "How come you kept this place a secret from me?"

Evangeline would have answered but she had a six inch rib at her mouth chewing off the delicious pork.

They finished the ribs and Martha was there at once to remove the tray and replace it with ice cold slices of rich red watermelon.

"I must be dead and this is heaven!" Spur said. Martha grinned and left them to their dessert.

Walking back to the Evangeline saloon, he pondered about telling Evangeline exactly what he was trying to do. He decided not to, not yet. He had a few more night watches to make first. He would go to the sheriff and Evangeline and the newspaper man as the last resort. The way things were looking, he just might have to do that soon.

At the Evangeline she ushered him to the foot of the stairs up to her quarters and held out her hand.

"Mr. McCoy, I had a delightful afternoon and evening. We should do this again, one of these days."

"I ate enough to last me a week," Spur said.

"So we'll make it in a week." She smiled. "Unless you get hungry before then."

She took a step upward and turned. She was eye to eye with him. She smiled.

"Mr. McCoy. Would you do me one small favor?"

"Of course, Miss Evangeline."

She leaned toward him her eyes closed and touched his lips to his. He didn't touch her with his hands. She never touched him. Their lips clung together for precious moments, then she eased away from him.

It took a moment for her eyes to come open, and she put out a hand which he caught to steady her.

She crinkled up her nose and the twin dimples popped inward on her cheeks. Her black eyes sparkled.

"Well now, that was nice." She turned abruptly. "Good night, Mr. McCoy. Perhaps we can do this again one of these nights." Then she walked up the steps and did not look back. When she stepped inside the door above, Spur McCoy went out of the saloon and back to his room at the Aspen Hotel. He found it empty, put the chair handle under his locked door and waited until just after midnight. Then he slid out his window to the hitch-roof and down to the ground.

It took him ten minutes to find a good spot to

watch the front door of the newspaper office. Then he settled down and waited. He checked the position of the Big Dipper, and when the movement of the Dipper around the North Star told Spur that it was four a.m. he rose, stiff and sore and walked back to the hotel.

He didn't want to bother climbing in his window, but the door was locked and braced with the chair. He got inside without attracting attention and slept until eight-thirty the next morning.

8

Willard Kleaner walked past the Carson Hotel as he did every morning on his way to work at his uncle's Aspen Hotel. This morning he stopped and stared, then recovered and kept moving so as not to attract attention.

Two desperados reined in at the hitching rack in front of the Carson, dismounted and tied up. Slowly and with seeming pain, they eased their saddlebags off the mounts, took blanket rolls and small crushed carpetbags from their tie down spots behind saddles and limped into the Carson Hotel. They had been on a long, rugged ride, Willard could tell.

Willard knew what they were at once. He could recognize the type anywhere. They definitely were bank robbers who had been on the run for several days, weeks maybe, and were here to hide out, get a hot bath and eat some good food for a change.

It was like in *Ranger Dale and the Robber's Roost*. Ranger Dale hadn't been sure about the robbers at first, but he had tracked them down quickly. This pair looked about as worn out as the outlaws in the book had been. Neither showed any signs of a gunfight wound, but both were heavily bearded—the two week kind, not a three or six months beard. Their hair was shaggy; they were dirty and their clothes worn and torn.

The nags they rode in on looked ready for the glue factory somewhere, Willard decided. He hurried past the Carson, to the Aspen Hotel and asked the room clerk if he'd seen Mr. McCoy come down.

McCoy was in the dining room having breakfast. Willard hurried in and stood there in front of the table, turning his small bill cap in his hands. When McCoy looked up, Willard was ready.

"Sir, you said to come to you again if I saw something . . ."

Spur put a finger across his lips, and Willard stopped.

"But you said . . ."

"Not here. Out in the lobby." Spur put down his napkin on the bones of his breakfast, and they went into the lobby where Spur eased onto a soft couch and Willard sat beside him.

"I saw two of them. They just got into town and went into the Carson Hotel. A mangy, beat up pair of desperados they are, Mr. McCoy."

Spur's eyes twinkled but he tried not to let the boy see it. He listened as Willard gave detailed descriptions of both men, ages, height, weight, and what they wore.

"No sense setting around here, Willard. Let's go and see if we can find them. Chances are they registered at the hotel and left right away heading to the closest bar for something to drink."

Spur and Willard left by the side door, then Spur

checked the saloon across the street from the Carson
Hotel. It was closed so early in the morning. Down
the street three doors was another saloon with the
door standing open. Inside, Spur found the pair at
the stand-up bar of rough lumber. Sawdust on the
floor absorbed the spilled whiskey, spit and now and
again, blood.

The men were precisely as Willard had described.
With a jolt, Spur stared at the taller man. "Abe
Varner!" Spur whispered. He hadn't seen Varner
since he was last in Kansas. Varner had cheated a
hangman in a small county seat when three of his
friends rode in with guns blazing, killed the sheriff
and one deputy and got away clean.

Abe Varner was a bank robber, and had killed half
a dozen men in the process. He could have only one
purpose for being in Johnson Corners.

Spur did not know the other man, but he was a
match for Varner in style and appearance. A two
man gang of bank robbers was better than doing it
alone. The barkeep stood in front of Spur.

"Yeah, got any Rough Cut chawing tobacco?"

The apron brought out a plug and tossed it on the
counter. Spur tossed him a quarter in return and left
the saloon. The purchase made him just another
customer. Abe Varner would not think it unusual.
The killer was smart, clever. That was why he had
stayed alive so long.

This assignment might turn out to be more than
just a hunt for a missing man after all.

Spur eased outside and motioned to Willard.
"You're right, son, at least one of those men is a
wanted killer, and a bank robber. They've probably
been on the road for a long time. I'll watch them for
a while."

Spur grinned and slapped Willard on the back.

"Hey, that was really good, smart thinking to peg these guys. There could be a reward in this. Now get back to work."

Spur leaned against the clothing store front wall and kept the saloon door in sight. He felt uneasy. He should be working on his other two problems, not taking on a new one. Now he had three cases, not one.

At least there was no mystery about Abe Varner. No mistaking him for someone else. A cold blooded killer with no conscience. Spur had to decide if he would take him into custody right now or see what he was up to. There could be four or five more men outside of town letting Varner set it up and then they would all swoop down on the bank.

Spur wandered down the boardwalk and looked across the street at the Concord Bank. Two doors, one in front, one in back and lots of windows. If he were going to rob it he'd want at least four men. He pondered the idea of telling the sheriff and the banker.

Spur decided to tell neither one. He would watch the pair and if the robbers tried to take the bank, he would hit back so hard they wouldn't know what to do.

As he stood across the street from the bank, he saw the pair of robbers coming down the boardwalk on his side. Spur found a chair and leaned back against a storefront.

Varner and his friend passed within six feet of Spur. His hat was pulled down over his eyes, letting him see out, but not offering anyone a look at him.

Both robbers studied the bank as they walked past. They ankled across the street and went by the money pit close up, pausing as if going inside. Spur figured they had the place well reconnoitered already.

He followed them up the street and watched them go into the Carson Hotel. Something about Varner he was trying to remember. Then he had it. Varner liked to attack a bank just before closing time, when the workers and any guards were tired.

He'd take it just before the vault was closed for the night, so he had fewer problems getting to the money. After the hit on the bank he would charge away and could get lost in the darkness. That was the way Spur remembered Varner had worked before. This time he would have some surprises.

Spur sat down on the edge of the boardwalk just down from the Carson hostelry. A year ago a flash flood had poured down through Main Street, gouging out tons of loose dirt. When they got it leveled off again, the street was eighteen inches below the boardwalks in some spots.

Spur checked a grandfather clock in the Johnson Corner jeweler's window. It was only a little after ten in the morning. He figured the pair would eat again soon, then have a sleep and be ready to take the bank at 2:45.

Spur pushed away from the boardwalk and ambled across the street to Moon's General Store. He did not go into Priscilla's store. She could be bothersome.

In the store he picked out a double barreled shotgun and a box of shells with double ought buck loads. The shots were the same size as a .32 pistol slug, from eight to thirteen in each round depending on the length. He took the long ones and distributed the shells in all of his pockets.

Nothing so effective for close in fighting like a

scatter gun and double ought buck. If he ran the army, every army unit in Indian country would arm every second man with a shotgun.

Spur arranged with Bill Moon to let him leave the unloaded shotgun just inside the store door, and meandered down the block. The Concord State Bank was situated in mid block, with only a front and rear door.

He leaned against the barber shop wall and speculated. If he covered the front, they could go in that way and out the back and down the alley. Get away clean. If he tried to cover the back he left the front open.

Spur had to get help or confide to the banker his suspicions and wait inside the bank. He didn't trust the sheriff because he knew nothing about him. Now there wasn't time to find out. He'd go with the banker.

Spur walked into the bank at two o'clock and talked with the president and owner, Barton Concord.

"Ah, Mr. McCoy. How are you finding our small town?"

"Dangerous," Spur said with an edge in his voice. "Could I talk to you privately?"

They went into the banker's office. As soon as the door shut Spur checked out the window. He did not see Varner or his partner.

"I think your bank is going to be robbed today, Mr. Concord. I'm a special lawman from the U.S. government in town looking for a murder suspect. I recognized the two men. If they act the way they have in the past, they will come in just before the bank closes at three and take it over."

"The sheriff! I'll call him."

"No, there isn't time. And if Varner spots anything out of the ordinary, he'll walk on by. Don't even tell your clerks. I'll be here with a shotgun and back both of them down. You can disarm them and then, we'll call the sheriff."

"Don't like guns in my back."

"Maybe you'd rather let them clean out your safe and your teller cages."

"No . . . no. That's what we pay the sheriff for. We should let him know."

"Tell him if you want to, but if you do, I'm going back to my hotel room. I'm trying to do you a favor."

Concord began to sweat. He wiped the moisture from his forehead and looked at the window, then at crossed infantry sabers on the wall.

"I had enough of fighting and killng in the war." At last he shrugged. "All right. If you think it's best. I just don't want any of my people getting hurt. Money can be replaced. My people can't."

Spur nodded. "I'll get my shotgun and come in the back door in five minutes. You have it open for me."

When Spur came up the alley to the bank a few minutes later, the banker stood outside waiting. He unlocked the door and they went inside. Spur unwrapped the new shotgun and pushed two rounds into the barrels.

Inside the bank, Spur looked for a hiding place. There was no spot in front of the cages. He'd have to be behind them, which would be a little awkward. It all depended how many men Varner had. The more he thought of the layout, the more he figured there would be only two men.

At least that's how Spur would do this bank.

Come in at 2:58, pull the door shade, lock it and take over the place. Tie up customers and workers, clean out the cash and leave by the back door.

With Varner you could never tell. He had a reputation of getting into trouble by shooting too much. A "wanted" flyer said the man simply enjoyed killing. That worried Spur. If there were only two men, Spur had a chance.

He found his spot, a small storage closet at the far side of the safe with a door that opened outward. Spur could leave the door ajar a crack and see everything going on. He told Concord who agreed. Spur asked Concord to be in his office with the door shut at closing time.

The clock moved. When it was a quarter of three, Spur pulled the closet door shut to a thin crack and put four shotgun shells in his right pocket where he could get to them quickly.

At five minutes to three the clerk and the two tellers were watching the number of people in the bank. They rushed to get most of them out by the three o'clock closing. None of them knew why Spur was in the closet.

When the clock hit three and struck, the head teller took his ring of keys and went to the door. Just as he reached the key for the lock, strong arms slammed the door open, jolting the teller off his feet.

Two men rushed into the bank, six-guns out. One turned and closed and locked the door. The other waved his gun at the two customers and the other employees.

"No heroes, and nobody gets hurt!" Abe Varner said loudly but in a controlled voice. "Tellers, clear out your money drawer and put it all on the marble in front of you. Do it now!"

The second man left the door and ran around the counter to the vault and saw that the big door was still open. He charged inside and began dumping money into a white flour sack he took from his belt.

Varner scowled at the customers.

"You, old man, lay down on the floor, on your face. Do it, right now." Varner watched as the man slowly knelt and then went to the floor.

"Miss, you too, on your back, next to him." She sat down then lay on the floor and shivered, her eyes frightened.

"You two tellers, or whatever, out here, fast. Get down beside your buddy there. Anybody reach for a hideout and he's dead, y'hear?"

Varner edged toward the counter, scooped up all the money and bills and dropped them into his flour sack, then went around the end of the counter to help his partner in the safe.

Spur McCoy at last had a shot. The muzzle of the shotgun was only an inch out of the closet when Spur pulled the trigger. Half of the .32 caliber sized slugs caught Abe Varner in the chest, churned through his ribs and lungs and blew four inches of his backbone against the far window which shattered and sent shards of glass spraying into the street.

The robber in the vault fired his pistol out the big opening. He peered around the door from floor level, saw the smoke from the shotgun muzzle near the closet and put three rounds into the door as he zig-zagged to the protection of the counter, then rushed toward the back door.

Spur stormed out of the closet, triggered the second barrel of the scatter gun down the hallway, but the robber expected the move and had dropped behind a stack of boxes. He leaped up after the shot passed, fired three times with his pistol down the hallway at Spur and charged out the back door.

By the time Spur got to the door, all he saw was the hind quarters of the black horse rounding the end of the alley and heading out of town. Another horse, saddled and provisioned, had been tied to the back yard fence of the house on the other side of the alley.

The bank owner looked out the back door, his face pale and terrified.

"Call the sheriff and the undertaker!" Spur shouted. "I'm going after the other one!"

Spur vaulted into the saddle of the horse Varner had planned to use, pulled the reins loose and pounded the big gray down the alley after the second robber. He had left the shotgun in the hallway. Now all he had was his long barreled .45, and more than twenty useless shotgun shells.

9

Spur McCoy was a quarter of a mile out of town on the Denver Stage Road before he saw the robber again. The Secret Service agent topped a slight rise and looked down hill. The rider on the black had stopped near a large Douglas fir to check his back trail. When he saw Spur he cut into the timber along the trail and vanished.

The Denver Stage Road here followed a gentle downgrade to a valley below where it crossed and climbed upward higher than the community of Johnson Corners which rested at 6,235 feet.

Spur rode forward slowly. The thick fir, lodgepole pine and Engelmann spruce would serve as a perfect blind for bushwhacking. He pulled the gray off the road two hundred yards from where the robber vanished into the woods, and began working ahead at a walk.

He would try to cut the man's trail and track him. It would be simple in the soft footing of the forest floor, where decades of pine needles and leaves from the aspen had created a six-inch deep mulch.

He found the trail ten minutes later. The marks in the mulch showed that the rider was pushing his horse fast. Spur moved out on the trail, slowing when needed, but racing ahead when there was only one logical direction for the rider to take.

A half hour later the trail led across a small stream. Spur rode into the open not thinking about being shot at. Just as his horse stepped in the water a rifle cracked from less than fifty yards away, and the bullet whispered over Spur's head. The last step of the horse into foot deep water had pulled him downward to safety.

Spur jolted off the horse and raced to a pile of boulders on the near side of the stream. Three rifle slugs splattered granite as he ran but the lead missed. He had seen a rifle on board the borrowed horse, but he had no idea if there was a box of rounds for it.

It was no help now as his horse stood hock deep in the creek thirty feet away taking a long drink.

Another rifle round hit the rocks he lay behind. The angry lead ricocheted off into the timber. A bright sun began to slide behind the distant ridges of the Rocky Mountains. It would be dark in two hours.

Spur pulled his long barreled Colt and juked his head around the side of the rock to locate the smoke from the black powder. He saw it drifting from a thicket of brush just down wind from a solid looking aspen. He sighted in waist high to the left to the Aspen and fired.

His round brought two more slugs zinging over the rock. Then there was silence. Spur lifted the top of his low crowned brown hat over the rim of the rocks on the end of his pistol barrel. There was no reaction.

He whistled for his horse, but it had moved another twenty feet away from him to the far bank and grazed on some new grass. Varner had not trained the animal to come on call. So, all he had to do was run to the horse and use her as a cover to get into the timber.

That could be deadly if the robber was still around.

Only one way to find out.

Who wanted to live forever?

As the Indians said: This was a good day to die.

Spur held his Colt ready, surged away from the rocks and raced for the horse which went right on munching.

No shots slammed through the cool, high mountain air at him.

McCoy grabbed the reins, stepped into the saddle and rode hard into the fringe of aspens and small fir bordering the stream.

When he was safely into the woods he stopped and listened. The only thing he could hear was the scream of a large red tailed hawk, and then the wind blowing through the seventy and eighty foot high, old growth conifers.

The outlaw had seen his leader killed, he would understand the rules of the game. His horse had been loaded for a long ride. But would he choose to run or to fight? In another two hours he could escape into darkness without fear of being followed.

Spur would have to wait for morning to pick up his trail and by then he would be forty miles away. The robber had all the advantages: he could fade away in the darkness, he could stand and fight, he could try to bushwhack Spur again, he could ride around in circles until Spur gave up and went back to town.

Somehow Spur felt the man would fight. He had the looks of a fighter. He had seen his partner gunned down and might want revenge. He would shoot from hiding if he could arrange it, and in these mountains and timber it would be easy to do.

Spur cut the trail quickly this time and saw that the horseman was not galloping. The black had been held to a walk and to Spur's surprise the trail turned back toward town. They were less than two miles from Johnson Corners. Why would he go back that way?

As Spur followed the trail, the answer came quickly. The rider crossed a rushing stream that was thirty feet wide and belly deep on the horse, then angled into the upper end of the valley the stream had carved. It was strewn with horse sized boulders.

There was a forest of them, and few trees, as if the boulders had grown here instead of trees. The soil was sandy and thin. No wonder no Douglas firs decided to thrive here.

He paused at the start of the valley of boulders, then saw the glint of sun off metal and dropped off his horse, pulled out the rifle, an 1866 Winchester .44. He had always liked these guns. Varner had picked well.

The weapon was 43 inches long with a tubular magazine that held 12 rim fire cartridges. Loaded the rifle weighed nine pounds. But it could fire 13 rounds without reloading. It was a newer model of the old Henry .44. Spur checked the chamber and there was a round in place. In the saddle bag he found two boxes of the .44 caliber rifle sounds. He dumped a dozen of them in his pocket and tied the horse to a bush.

Then Spur began moving forward through the big rocks toward where he had seen the rifle flash at him in the sun. It was slow going.

Spur kept track of his direction by a twin topped Engelmann spruce near the end of the short valley. Once he scaled a boulder that had a chunk broken out. For two minutes he peered over the top of the granite hoping to see movement, but there was none. He had not seen the man's horse.

He figured the outlaw had tied his horse in the woods at the far end of the valley, and worked back into the rocks to a good spot for a ten yard ambush where he couldn't miss.

That was what Spur feared he might try.

He came around the side of a boulder nearly as big as a house, and twenty feet ahead saw the back of a man vanish around another big rock. Spur waited. The Jasper might backtrack. The Winchester was ready to fire. He sighted in on the boulder and the one past that and waited.

Nothing.

Spur moved again, rushing forward to the next cover, the rock the killer had just left. For the flash of a second Spur heard a noise and looked up. The robber was on top of the rock less than six feet away! Spur lifted the Winchester and fired. The unaimed round skidded off the stone breaking up and splattered some of its hot lead into the robber who dropped out of sight.

"Don't be a fool," Spur called. "You're hurt and I'll kill you if I have to just like I did Varner. You ready to die?"

There was no answer.

The stick of dynamite with a short fuse sailed over the granite boulder and Spur dove away from it, rolling as far as he could toward the open space behind the rock.

The blast went off with a cracking roar.

Dynamite in the open makes a furious sound and concussion, but without shrapnel behind it the effectiveness is minimal. Spur shook his head and lifted up, a fresh round in his Winchester.

He could see no movement.

Slowly he edged around the big boulder, every nerve ending alert and tingling, ready to report any sight, sound or touch of the enemy.

Around the boulder Spur found a few spots of blood and an empty rifle cartridge. That was all.

He looked ahead. More big rocks.

A rifle bullet splattered off the rock just past him, and Spur dove to the side away from the sound of the shot and crouched behind a smaller rock. The robber had angled to the left instead of moving forward. Spur searched for the blue smoke that gave away the gunman's position. He found it but there was no target.

As he watched, the robber lifted up and fired again. Spur had time only to duck before the slug slammed into his protective rock. He reached up and fired his pistol at the position in a purely defensive move.

Then there was silence in the high country.

Spur wished he had made up some small dynamite bombs before he came—except he didn't know he was coming. He had found that by taping roofing nails to a stick of dynamite with a short fuse, he had an effective grenade that he could throw a hundred feet while the fuse burned.

Now he saw the robber move toward the woods. Spur fired twice with the rifle at the retreating figure. Where was he going? Where was his horse?

On foot the man would be much easier to run to ground. He seemed to be working toward the left of the small valley. Spur stopped trying to shoot the man and ran flat out toward the far end of the valley less than a hundred yards away now. He slanted far to the left hoping to come out in the trees well before the robber did.

He heard only one more shot which he figured was defensive, and then he left the last boulder and rushed twenty yards across an open meadow into the brush and aspen and fringes of young fir trees in the open where the sun could nourish them.

He paused a moment, made sure he had a new round in the Winchester, then jogged forward through the edge of the woods. Where had the man left his horse?

Spur heard a nicker, ahead, and edged around a big spruce and saw the horse tied to an aspen. It took him a moment to find the position he wanted. He was ten yards from the mount, and slightly behind it, but with a good field of fire toward the edge of the valley.

Spur lay down beside a huge Douglas fir, sighted in just past he horse and waited.

It was two or three minutes before Spur heard the man coming. He swore softly, and used his rifle as a crutch as he limped around the last boulder, took a long look behind him and then hobbled toward the brush.

Spur tracked him, waited until he entered the woods and turned toward the horse. Spur wanted to take him back alive, to put him on trial. He lowered his sights, aimed at the injured left leg and squeezed off the round.

The crack of the Winchester caught the man totally by surprise. He had no time to move before the heavy .44 caliber slug tore into his left thigh, spun him backward and dumped him into the mulch in plain sight.

"Drop the iron!" Spur bellowed. "Drop it and put up both hands or you're buzzard food in about ten seconds."

Slowly the man's hands came up.

He sat up then, his face a twisted, angry mask of pain.

"Yeah, yeah! Don't shoot no more. I don't want to die. Just get me to a doctor!"

"Throw out your pistol!"

"Right, yes." A six-gun came out of leather slowly and the man tossed it away from him. He pushed the rifle butt first toward Spur so the trigger was well out of his reach.

"Hands high!" Spur demanded. He lifted up, keeping the robber in his sights and moved forward slowly. The wounded man made no try to move.

"I'm bleeding to death!" the robber shouted.

Spur moved quicker then, checked the robber for a hidden derringer, then put down his rifle and examined the thigh wound. It was bleeding too much. Spur took the neckerchief from the robber and pushed it against the back of his leg where the round had exited.

"Hold it there," Spur said. He took his own big red handkerchief and tied it tightly around the leg, pressing the compress in place to stop the flow of blood. The lead splatter wounds in his lower leg were not serious. They had stopped bleeding.

"Nothing broken," Spur said. "You're damn lucky I didn't blow you in half in the bank."

"The way you did Abe?"

"Yes, you were next. What's your name?"

"George Washington."

"Sure. Well, George, I bet the sheriff has a broadside or two on you. Teaming up with Varner means you've got a wanted for you from somewhere. Now, get on your horse, unless you want to walk."

It took them nearly two hours to get back to Johnson Corners. Darkness had fallen, but they rode the last mile on the Stage Road.

Spur tied both horses in front of the Sheriff's Office and found a deputy waiting for him.

"Trouble?" the deputy asked.

"No we were on a picnic and got stung by hornets. Where's the sheriff? Tell him I've got a prisoner for him over at Doc Slocum's."

Spur and his prisoner went on to the doctor's office where the medic checked the wound and at once cut off the robber's pant leg and went to work.

He seemed to know what he was doing. He probed the wound to make sure the bullet all came out. The second probe with a long wire like tool made the robber pass out.

"Easier this way," Doc Slocum said. "I don't hold with that fancy ether stuff that's coming out." He doused all the wounds with carbolic and then wrapped them up with clean white bandages. White tape completed the job.

Sheriff Phillip Gump knocked on the door and came in. He looked at Spur, then at the prisoner.

"This the other bank robber?" the lawman asked.

"Seems to be, what's left of him," Doc Slocum said.

"Can I put him in jail?"

"Sure if the county wants to pay me to change his dressing every two days. There or here."

In his pocket, Spur found a gold one dollar piece smaller than a dime and handed it to the medic.

"On his account," Spur said. Then nodded at the lawman. "Peers I need to talk to you about that other robber. You have a paper for me to sign?"

"Yep. You better come down to the office with this hombre and we'll get it done. Ain't often we have a bank robbery where a stranger knows about it in advance and guns down the robbers."

"Knew Abe Varner from before, Sheriff. Never seen this one though. Says he's George Washington."

The sheriff snorted, picked up the unconscious man, hoisted him over his shoulder and carried him out the door. Spur McCoy followed.

He paused. "Oh, Doc. There's two horses at the rail out front. Used to belong to two bank robbers. I'd think the county will transfer all rights to you for medical services. Livery can probably buy them from you." Spur grinned and left to catch up with the sheriff. He had some explaining to do.

10

Spur sat across the desk from the big lawman and showed him the thin sheet of parchment he took from between pieces of a thick card in his wallet. The letter detailed Spur's position as a member of the U.S. Secret Service, and that he had jurisdiction in all matters local, county, territorial, state, and federal.

The parchment was signed by the President of the United States, U.S. Grant, and William Wood, director of the Agency. A two inch embossed seal took up half the page.

Sheriff Gump handed the parchment back to Spur. He folded it and inserted it between the halves of the heavy cardboard backed picture and put it away in his wallet.

"Nobody but you can know about this, Sheriff," Spur said softly. "I still have a job to do here."

"Yes, fine with me. I always cooperate with the

federal authorities, especially now that we're a state. Anything I can do to help you?"

"My real job here is not as violent as this one turned out to be. If I need help, I'll sure call on you. This other matter is much more delicate."

"I'm always here."

Spur stood. "There is something else, Sheriff. I never would have known either of the robbers were in town if it hadn't been for a young man here. His name is Willard Kleaner."

"He told you about them?"

"Certainly did. Is there any kind of wanted posters on the men? If there are any dead or alive papers, he should be the one to get the reward on Varner."

"I'll look into it."

"Oh, I'd also like to set up a twenty-five dollar good citizen award for Willard, just in case nothing else comes through. It would go with a letter of commendation from you, as sheriff."

The sheriff chuckled. "He's the one who sent me on a wild goose chase once. Guess he was right this time. I'll arrange it."

Spur handed him a gold double eagle and a good five dollar bill.

"Be much obliged, Sheriff. Now, seems to me, I missed supper somewhere along the way."

Spur went back to his room, washed up and changed clothes, then walked downstairs to the dining room and had a steak dinner and two desserts. By the time he finished it was after eight o'clock.

He went back up the stairs wondering if he should go over to the Envangeline for a hand of poker, or if he should watch the printing plant again. That had to be the key, but so far he was at a dead end on the counterfeiting and the right identity of George Slocum was the killer from Washington, D.C.

He came through the lobby and started up the stairs when he saw Priscilla Davis. She smiled at him and he nodded. She went up the steps after he did, and then hurried down the hallway as he opened his door.

"I've been waiting for you, Mr. McCoy," she said softly. "I knew you would come."

She looked up and down the hall, and when she saw no one, she stepped into his room and tugged him inside, then closed the door.

"I couldn't wait to see you again! Spur McCoy you simply set me on fire, do you know that?"

"Miss Davis, I don't think you should be here. Your reputation."

"Oh, poo. I don't give a whit about that. What good is a reputation? It can't keep you warm at night? It can't make love to you." She wore a short jacket over a full skirted dress. She pulled the jacket off and Spur was amazed to see that the top of the dress had been folded down. Nothing covered her breasts.

"You like my titties, you told me you did. Please pet them. Please kiss me!"

She walked toward him slowly. "I don't ask much. Just use me however you want. Strip me or just push up my dress. You don't even have to take your pants off if you want it fast and rough . . ."

Spur held out his hands as she walked toward him. He caught her shoulders and kept her away.

"No, Priscilla. I don't think so. You want too much. What happened to the story about the man who wanted you pregnant?"

"Oh, poo. Did you believe that? I made that up so you would be nice to me, so you would make love to me. Was that so bad? I love to make love. Don't you?"

"Well, yes, but I'm a man."

"So, I'm a woman. I love it as much as you do. More I think, yes, definitely more." She threw the jacket to one side and reached behind her to open some snaps and hooks and then pulled the dress over her head.

Priscilla stood before him naked. Her lovely breasts shook for a moment, and then began a small dance as she walked toward him.

"Priscilla, don't you understand?"

Her hands fumbled at his belt. One massaged the long hard lump forming quickly in back of his fly. "Oh, he likes it! He likes to see my titties and my muff of crotch hair. He wants inside! I just know he wants inside me!"

Spur backed up again, tripped over the chair and fell on the bed on his back. Priscilla was on top of him in the blink of an eye. Suddenly he was laughing.

"You are persistent," he said from his back. He felt her hands rubbing his erection through his pants. Then she began opening the buttons on his fly.

"Am I sexy too?"

"Yes, extremely sexy."

"You want to do it with me?"

"Do what?"

"Make love . . . fuck three or four times."

He watched her. Her hands fought through fabric and closed around his erection.

"Do you want him inside me?"

McCoy groaned. He was only a man, not a saint. The woman had problems, but it wasn't up to him to solve them. Right now he had a rather insistent case of swelling that she could relieve.

"Hey, big cock, you want him inside my warm hole?"

Slowly Spur nodded.

She grinned. Spur rolled her over and spread her legs wide and thrust forward. He knew his pants would chafe her. He knew that he was fully clothed and that it might hurt her. But he found her heartland and stabbed and burst past the tightness, then he slid into a lubricated sheath that accepted him.

At once her legs came up around his waist, then his armpits where she locked them together.

"Darling, make this first one so fast you'll be ready for more!"

Spur grunted and drove forward. He was so on fire he hardly thought about her. He panted and humped her and drove hard and fast and let only his own desires guide him. For a moment he worked it up, then he paused letting the thrill remain, but pushing it slowly away. Then he moved her legs so they rested on top of his shoulders and he arched his back and pounded his hips like a pile driver slamming his cock into her juicy slit.

She took all he could offer and thrust to meet him as he powered higher and higher.

Faster and faster, harder and harder, and Spur pounded his own music, with not even a thought of the woman. Then the dam broke and the surge swept downstream and carried him along as his hips slammed harder and harder, moving him deeper and deeper until at last he exploded with a dozen hard thrusts, each one tougher and deeper than the last.

Then he eased her legs down and fell on top of her spent half dead.

She let him rest for five minutes, then moved and he rolled off her, flat on his back.

She sat up and watched him. "Nice, good. You're good at making love. You have anything up here to drink?"

He took a pint of whiskey from a drawer. He kept the bottle for medicinal purposes, but since neither of them had been shot it was not needed as an antiseptic. He mixed a drink of whiskey with the cool water from the ceramic pitcher and she downed half of it.

"I think I like your place here," she said. "I'll have to come back every night."

"I'd be good for two nights, then you'd have to bury me."

She shook her head. "Your big rod just gets harder and harder the more he's used. I should know. Is it my turn yet?"

"Not until you take my clothes off."

"Hell, I can do that easy."

It took her all of two minutes to strip him naked, then she grinned as she inspected him as he lay on the bed, one foot on his lifted knee, and his hands under his head.

"I know just how I'm going to do it," she said and sat on his stomach.

"Up there?"

"Yes, up here. I've . . . I've never been done this way."

"You have to do most of the doing."

"Good, show me how."

"First there's a basic male requirement before anything very sexy can happen."

"Oh," she said. She scooted down and lifted up and moved until she sat on his legs.

"What a poor little, sad, soft worm."

"That's a whip, lady."

"He's a worm who dreams of being a lance. Can I make him into a lance?"

She could, and did.

A few minutes later, Priscilla squealed as she lowered herself gently on his shaft as she held it upright.

"My god, this even *feels wicked!*" she whispered. "I want to do it all night this way!"

She settled down until her round bottom hit his pelvic bones, then she squealed in delight and looked at him. "Why didn't you tell me there were other ways to make love? I need to know them all. Will you teach me?"

"Sorry, I'm not a qualified teacher. I'm sure you do all right all by yourself." He didn't have to tell her what to do next. She instinctively lifted up and dropped down on him, then she built up a rhythm and slowly angled forward until she was riding him like a pony.

"Lordy but this is wild!" Priscilla crooned. "Whyn't anybody show me this before?"

"Probably didn't know you had the talent for it," Spur said, then he felt the woman start to climax and she fell on top of him shaking and vibrating and spasming like she was having a fit, then she smiled and went through the same series of spasms again before she trailed off and lay still. He was sure she was sleeping.

The one eye opened. "Hell no, I ain't sleeping, big stick. Just loving every second of it. You know I'm thinking of moving to a new town and opening up myself a fancy ladies house. Think I could make a go of it?''

"Just don't steal all the trade away from your girls, Priscilla." Spur gave a pair of grunting strokes and shot his load and rolled her away from him. Spur got up and began dressing.

"Thought you said I could stay all night?"

"I didn't even say you could come inside. Now get dressed or I'll set you in the hall bare assed naked."

"Don't see why you hate me, Spur McCoy."

"I don't hate you, Priscilla. I have some work to get done before the sun comes up. And it doesn't involve a pretty woman. So hustle your bones."

She dressed and was ready when he was.

"You and me make a good team, don't we? I'll be back every night you want me. Or you could come up to my house. I really don't live behind the store. Pa left me a nice place, three bedrooms, we could use all three beds every night!"

Spur grabbed her shoulders and stared at her sternly. "Priscilla. I told you, I have work to do. It's serious work and I don't have time to play sexy games with you every night. I hope you realize that."

"Anything you say, Spur. But you can put that spur of yours in my cunny just anytime you want!"

Spur shook his head and led her to the door. He had strapped on his .45 and took his hat. He checked the hallway and when it was clear he pushed her out and told her to go down the steps. He'd used the back stairs to protect her reputation.

When he was sure she was gone, Spur slid out the door, locked it and went down the back steps.

He walked quickly to the alley behind the newspaper and found a window that would be lighted if anyone worked at the press.

For two hours he sat there watching. Nothing happened. He stood, stretched and walked two blocks to get the kicks out of his legs. Then he leaned against a fence and watched for three more hours before he gave it up. There was nothing going on at the printing plant. That meant Doc had all the bills made up he needed. He could be sliding them into use a few at a time, as he needed them.

Spur walked the three blocks down to Doc Slocum's office. The place was dark. No reason any lights should be on here. He had taken care of the emergency and was probably in bed by now.

Spur went past the Evangeline saloon and found it open. Only a half dozen gamblers played at two tables. Evangeline sat at her elevated table nursing a beer. Spur stopped beside her table and pointed at a chair. She nodded.

"Out kind of late, aren't you for a hero who saved all of our money at the bank. Let me buy our hero a beer."

She signalled the barkeep who brought a bottle of beer. Spur thanked her and pulled at it.

"I thought you might be in for another poker game," she said.

"I got tied up on another project. But I've still got you on my list. I never let a woman beat me at pocker."

"Lots of women are expert gamblers, me for one."

"But I never let a man beat me at poker, either. I'm not prejudiced."

She laughed and sipped at her beer. Then watched him a moment. "Spur McCoy, you're not in town to buy a business. I figured that out the first day you were here. You're not a real businessman. There's an aura about you, a quality, an animal-like tenseness, an alertness like you expect to be shot at the next second or two.

"You try to hide it, to be casual, but I've seen it before. I used to know a gunfighter who was the same way, and a sheriff who could never turn it off.

"When you went after those bank robbers, I finally realized that you're a lawman. Just what kind, I don't know. And I certainly haven't figured what you're after here in town. Fact is, I don't care much, as long as it isn't me."

She smiled at him and lifted her beer.

"How did I do? Am I about right?"

11

Secret Service Agent McCoy watched the small, delicate gambler in the Evangeline gaming house, and a slow smile spread across his face.

"Lady Gambler, you just pushed all of your chips into the pot, are you sure that you've won?"

"I've got a royal flush, I don't see how you can beat me."

Spur reached out and put his big paw over her small hand. "You win, but don't tell anyone. I still have some work to do in town and I need to be incognito."

She laughed softly. "Hey, you can go to cognito if you want to or stay here. I won't tell a soul. You still haven't told me what kind of a lawman you are." Her eyes sparkled and her twin dimples popped inward.

"Probably won't until I get things cleared up. You playing any black jack tonight?"

She took out the cards from the drawer in her

desk. Spur picked them up and checked the sides, then the face. He smiled and put them back.

"Could you tell if the cards had been shaved or marked?"

"Can an unweaned calf find his mamma in a herd of a hundred cows?"

Spur put the four phony five dollar bills on the table and pushed one to the center of the table. She dealt a hand and he won with a twenty to her eighteen. He pulled a five and played again. At the end of twenty minutes Spur had lost the four five dollar bills.

"Take a look at those greenbacks," Spur said softly. She looked at them.

"Are they good currency?"

"I never notice bills much." She shrugged. "Feel good."

"Check the serial numbers."

"Oh, my god! They're all the same. Then they must be counterfeit. All bills are supposed to have different numbers on them, aren't they?"

Spur flipped a twenty dollar gold piece on the table and took the four fake fives back.

"Just don't tell anybody about this either. It's what I'm working on. Don't let on, don't refuse fivers, or tell your aprons to watch for them. I don't want any tip off to the counterfeiter."

She smiled, and reached over and touched his hand. "Thanks for trusting me. I might have a printing press in the back room turning these out myself."

"You don't, I checked."

Evangeline laughed. "You did not."

Spur stood. "Past my bed time. I better move on."

"Thanks for the game, I'm still ahead."

"I'll get even, next time."

"Good, there will be a next time."

Spur nodded at her and then walked out the saloon door. He found few people on the street. Nothing unusual. He went into his hotel, up to the second floor and then looked for the stairs to the roof. He found it at the far end of the hall.

Without much trouble, he picked the lock and went up the dusty stairs to the roof. The stars were out and in this high country they looked close enough to pick and put in a diamond pouch.

He went to the parapet built around the rooftop and leaned on it watching the town. All of the businesses below except two saloons were closed and dark. A few stragglers left the watering holes, then even they closed.

Spur spotted one figure leaving the Johnson Mercantile, it was Priscilla. She went down the street toward some residences and vanished in the gloom of the quarter moon.

A deputy sheriff made his rounds, routinely trying doors on the businesses, walking slowly, sure how many times he would make the circuit before dawn.

Spur saw a flare of light down near Doc Slocum's house, then the rattle of a buggy as one, one-horse rig followed another down the street and out the Denver Stage Road. An emergency this time of night had to mean the imminent birth of a new citizen.

For a moment he thought he saw a flare of light near the newspaper office. Yes, it came again, then the sound of a door closing two blocks down. This might be important. Why would the newsman come back to his office after midnight? Spur left the roof, returned to the ground floor and out the rear door of the Aspen Hotel.

He came to the newspaper office quickly but found it as dark as it had been on his previous patrols.

Something had happened here. He went down the vacant lot beside the news plant and soon found a small shoulder high window. Spur looked inside. No lights showed.

He pushed on the double hung window and it was not locked, the wooden frame sliding upward easily. Spur found a wooden box and stood on it so he could squeeze through the opening and inside. He used a sulphur match to light his way, found a candle and began exploring the back shop of the newspaper.

The Secret Service agent found plenty of printing inks, even some green, but nothing that was suspicious. He explored the whole back shop, checking printing papers, but found none that could be used for making five dollar bills.

Spur checked the back door and saw that it was locked only by a bar across two iron holders. He lifted the bar and peered outside. Where were the telltale clues of the counterfeiter?

The rattling of the front door came through the silent building like a burglar alarm. Spur quickly blew out the candle, but he knew it was too late. Whoever it had been at the door must have seen the candlelight. He hurried to the back door and eased it open, before he could sprint away, a form came running around the corner brandishing a darkly silent pistol.

Spur froze against the inside of the door, counting on the lawman or owner to charge into the darkness of the building interior.

For a moment the man outside hesitated. Then he struck a pair of matches, held them high and stepped inside the print plant.

Spur slashed at the hand with the matches with one fist, and powered his second down on the man's right hand that held the pistol.

The six-gun clattered to the floor and the matches died as Spur rushd past the other man into the alley and pounded fast down the length to Fourth Street and then up it to Main. He stopped running, went through another alley and walked quickly to the rear entrance to the Aspen Hotel.

Two minutes later he was in his hotel room where he locked and braced the door with a chair, then undressed in the dark and crawled into his empty bed.

Close.

At least he still had most of his cover story in place. But he had struck out again on the counterfeiting. If all else failed he would have to go to the bank and see if they could spot any deposit having large numbers of the bills included. One of the retail stores in town would be the best chance as the pipeline into the economy. Surely the doctor was working through someone else. The sawbones made so little in this town he could never circulate many of his counterfeit bills.

Spur rolled over and tried to go to sleep. He couldn't. There had to be something here that he was missing, something right under his nose that would give away the counterfeiter and tie down Doc Slocum's involvement. But what the hell was it?

Spur looked at his Waterbury at two-thirty by lighting a match. He checked again and it was four a.m. He must have slept part of the time, but he couldn't remember. When morning came at five-thirty and he rolled out so his feet hit the cold boards of the floor, he wondered if he had slept at all.

And still he had no idea where the right handles were to pull to find out what he needed to know.

He had a miserable breakfast in the cafe across the street. The waitress and cook were both mad at the world and so was he. When he got to the sheriff's office at eight that morning, the sheriff was cheerful and pleased.

"Worked up a right smart certificate, we did. Betty in the courthouse is good at making them things. Here want to see it?"

Sheriff Gump brought out a roll of stiff paper and spread it flat for Spur to read. It was hand printed with fancy lettering, old English he thought, and lots of scrolls and doo-dads around it. It read:

"Be it hereby known to all persons, that the Sheriff of Forest county, State of Colorado, does hereby applaud and commend one Willard Kleaner, fifteen years of age, for his part in recognizing two wanted felons and then alerting officials of the presence in our community of the two bank robbers.

"Said information by young Kleaner, his alertness and ability to convey such matter to friends and members of this department, did aid and abet and greatly help law officers to prevent the bank robbery and bring the desperados to justice.

"Willard Kleaner is hereby made the first official honorary Deputy Sheriff of Forest County by my order, and is entitled to all of the honors and privileges thereunto.

"The Sheriff's Department of Johnson County hereby awards William Kleaner the sum of twenty-five dollars, to reward him for his good citizenship. Drawn and dated this Seventeenth Day of June in the year of Eighteen hundred and Seventy-seven. By my order and hand . . . Sheriff Phillip Gump."

Spur handed it back. "Beautiful, Sheriff. Willard will treasure this award forever."

"Giving it to him at at little ceremony on the steps of the courthouse at ten this morning. I want you to be there."

"I'll be there, Sheriff. You find any wanted posters on either of the men?"

"Three on Varner, but no big cash reward. One hundred dollar one but I'd have to deliver his body to Tombstone, Arizona. I figure that's too far."

"Need nose plugs this time of year before you got him there. Put him on boot hill."

"Here we call it Culligan Swamp. Same idea. He'll be put down today." The sheriff hesitated. "How. . . how is your other problem coming along?"

"Slow. Too damn slow. But that's why they pay me this tremendous salary. I probably make about half of what you do." Spur walked to the door. "I'll keep you informed if this gets to the legal stage. I'm hoping somehow that it won't."

Spur turned to go out, then stepped back in the office. "Sheriff, you ever have any trouble with the woman who runs the Johnson Mercantile?"

"Priscilla Davis? Now and then. She seems to be settling down nicely to running the store. Quite a shock to her when her father died." He crinkled his brow. "Why?"

"Just a coincidence, I guess. She reminds me of somebody I used to know. Forget it, doesn't mean a thing."

Later that morning at the ceremony at ten o'clock, Zelda and Ronald Lewton stood proudly beside Willard as he was presented the certificate. It had been mounted in a frame that could be hung and had a piece of glass over it to protect it.

Two dozen people gathered around the steps as the sheriff made a little speech. Then the president of the bank, Barton Concord, gave a talk about how the future of the town was in the good hands of young men like Willard, and how proud he was of Willard and that he had opened a savings account at the bank in Willard's name with fifteen dollars already deposited in it.

More cheering followed that. But when the sheriff asked Willard to say something he just held up the frame and smiled. He was too overcome to say a word.

Ron Lewton had to help his wife back to the hotel. She was a bit unsteady on her feet and Spur figured she had some kind of illness. Willard ran ahead and showed the frame to everyone in the hotel, then put it on the wall until he could take it home and hang it in his room.

Spur McCoy stood on Main Street and looked at the newspaper plant and at Doc Slocum. What the hell was he going to do?

12

Willard Kleaner stood in the Aspen Hotel an stared at his certificate in the frame on the wall. It was the most wonderful thing that had ever happened to him. And he had forty dollars in hand! It was more money than he had ever owned . . . or even thought about.

He felt of the two crisp bills in his pocket and asked his uncle if he could take off a few minutes.

"I want to go to the bank, sir, to deposit my reward money in my new savings account."

"You best be paying attention to your work, boy. Not parading around with your money showing. Did you move that broke bed out of 104 and put the new one in?"

"No sir. That's my next project."

"You best be getting to it." Lewton paused. "I could hold that twenty-five dollars for you for safe-keeping."

Willard shook his head. "No sir. Thank you but I

want to keep it myself until I can deposit it. I never had twenty-five dollars before!" He hurried away toward the room on the first floor that needed the new bed. Some drunk had broken it the night before.

The idea grew slowly in Willard's mind as he worked the rest of the morning. At noon he ran all the way to the livery and talked to the man there. His name was Josh and he liked kids. He saw Willard coming and made a sound like a trumpet.

"Our local hero comes!" Josh said grinning.

"None of that," Willard said. "Just doing my . . . my civic duty the way every straight shooter should."

"Anyhow you rope it, cowboy, you done good. What's on your mind?"

"A horse. You got one for sale cheap?"

"How cheap?"

"Twenty dollars, horse, saddle, saddle blanket and bridle."

"You peer to be goin' somewhere?"

"No sir, Josh. I just want a horse of my own I can ride." He paused a moment. "I want to learn how to be a cowboy!"

Josh grinned. "In that case I might even give you some lessons. Come back here and lets look around. Might grub up something." He considered it a minute.

"Fact is, Doc Slocum sold me those two nags the bank robbers rode. The black is a valuable animal, but I could let you have the gray and her gear for twenty dollars."

"I'll take her!" Willard shrieked so delighted and excited that he could hardly talk normally.

Josh grinned. "Better look at her first. I might be pulling a fast one on you."

They examined the gray in a stall and Josh showed Willard the saddle, blanket, saddle bags and the bridle. There was also a lasso and Willard noticed that the saddle had a boot to hold a rifle.

"I think I want to buy her," Willard said. "About how old is she?"

Josh pulled the gray's lips apart and looked at her teeth.

"I'd say maybe eight or nine. Got fifteen good years left in her you take care of her. Oh, you got a place to keep her?"

"Sure have! My uncle has a little barn in back of his house. He keeps a horse there all the time. Plenty of room for two."

Willard held out the twenty dollar greenback. "You'll write me out a receipt won't you, so I have a bill of sale. I don't want to get my neck stretched for horse stealing."

Josh chuckled. "Sounds like you been reading them dime novels. I read one oncet in a while."

He eyed Willard. "You work over at the hotel, right? You come back after work and I'll have her saddled and ready. And with a bill of sale. You keep your greenback until then."

"Yes sir," Willard said. He walked up to the gray and patted her flank, then ran his hand along her back and scratched her ear. The gray turned toward him with big brown eyes.

"She looks like she wants a friend," Willard said.

Josh chuckled. "Guess so. Now she's found one. You come back this evening."

Willard ran back to the hotel. He had all his usual work done and started on the special things Uncle Ronald always had ready. At five-thirty he left and went to the stable. The gray was saddled and ready.

Willard gave Josh the twenty, accepted the bill of sale with his name on it and the date.

"You know how to get up on a horse?"

"Sure. Always the left side. That's the left when you're facing the same way the horse is. They get used to that, I don't know why."

"Right. Willard, you ever ridden before?"

"No sir. But I've read considerable about it."

"Can you get that saddle off?"

"Could you show me how?"

Josh grinned and demonstrated to Willard how to take the saddle off. Then he went through it step by step how to saddle up a mount. When he was through he pulled the saddle off and the blanket.

"Your turn," Josh said.

Willard put the saddle on correctly, and Josh waved him on his way.

The young man from Chicago could hardly believe it. He was on his own horse! He had a saddle and bridle and even saddle bags, and he was riding down the street of a Western town! It was almost more than he could accept. He held the reins loosely in his left hand, the way Billy Ringo did in *The Big Cattle Drive,* and let his right hand rest on his thigh, near where his .44 should be.

Wow! He had his own horse. He had not even thought what his uncle might say about it. Now his mount twisted. He could say whatever he wanted to, Willard knew for sure that he was keeping the gray. She didn't even have a name yet. She looked like a gray lady, a gray ghost. Yes! He would call her Ghost. That was a good name.

He rode down the side street, urged Ghost into a canter and almost shook himself to death. How in the world did you keep your bottom in the saddle when she was bouncing that way? Maybe Josh would give him some riding lessons, too.

Willard stopped Ghost in front of his uncle's house and tied the reins to the lilac bush and went inside.

He found his aunt in the living room, as usual. He watched her for a moment but she didn't even hear the screen door slam. She was too far into her wine bottle. Willard shrugged, went back outside and led Ghost around to the small barn and into the second stall. He gave her a feeding of oats and took off her saddle and bridle. She watched him with her big brown eyes. When she saw the oats she began eating.

Willard stayed there an hour, watching her, brushing her down with his uncle's brush. He didn't know if he did it right, but she liked the attention. When he went into the house it was almost dark.

His uncle was there. Aunt Zelda was not in the living room. Her husband had carried her into the bedroom again. It happened about half the time.

"Where you been, boy?" Ronald Lewton barked.

"Out in the barn feeding my new horse. You want to come see her. I call her . . ."

"Your what?"

"My new horse, Ghost. She's a gray, about the size of yours. I bought her today for twenty dollars."

"We'll take her back to Josh first thing in the morning."

Willard had never stood up to his uncle before. He was a half inch taller than the older man. Now he squared his shoulders and put a frown on his face.

"No. No, Uncle Ronald. I won't take Ghost back. She's mine. I bought her with my own money. You can't make me take her back!''

Ronald made the mistake of trying to hit his nephew. His hand shot out, but Willard pushed up his left hand to block it and his right hand tightened into a fist and he struck back.

His knuckles slammed into his uncle's jaw and staggered him back two steps.

"You hit me! You ungrateful child!"

"You tried to hit me first," Willard said. "And I'm not ungrateful. I just want to keep my horse."

"Who is going to buy feed for the animal?"

"I will. I can pay for it from that twenty dollars a month you get from my estate. The lawyer said it should come directly to me when I'm sixteen. That's in a couple of months."

"You know about . . ." Ronald Lewton felt a wave of loss sweep over him. He had been investing that twenty dollars a month at six percent and making a good return. How did the boy know about the financial . . .

"I'm going to keep Ghost, Uncle Ronald. If you won't let me keep her, I'll move out."

"You can't do that."

"I can. I can get a job at another hotel, or in a store. I'm big enough to work hard. I can earn twice what you pay me."

"Now, Willard. Don't jump to conclusions here. Of course you can keep the horse. Let's go see her. You paid how much for her? You got a saddle and bridle too. Well, well."

Ronald Lewton had never felt worse in his life. His wife was a drunk, his hotel was barely scraping by, and now his nephew was threatening to leave and take his twenty dollars a month with him. He would have to placate the boy somehow. At least until he was sixteen. Lordy, why did Zelda have to drink so much?

Spur McCoy sat and stared at his cards in Evangeline's. So far he had been there two hours after supper. He had lost twenty dollars and needed to get even.

It had been a worthless day. Most of the morning had been taken up with Willard and when he tried to dig into Doc Slocum's background in the afternoon, people clammed up like they had something to hide.

A customer in the general store laid it out for him.

"Look, we don't know you. We know Doc. He might not be the best doctor in the world, but he's all we got. We can't live here and take a sick child thirty miles to a doctor. Way I see it, we stick by Doc, least wise until we know for damned sure who you are and what you want."

Others said about the same thing. For the moment he forgot about the counterfeiter. One damn problem at a time. Unless they were the same problem. Spur got an idea what he could do the next day and he felt better.

He concentrated on his poker and a half hour later by playing conservatively and with the odds, he was ten dollars ahead. The barkeep brought him a note and Spur read it quickly.

"Now that you're ahead, come to my table and let me win it back." It was signed only with a capital "E."

Spur bowed out on the next hand and went around the saloon, then slid into the only other chair at the table on the slightly raised platform.

"Good evening, owner, general manager and top game playing lady," McCoy said.

When she looked up at him, Spur sucked in a quick breath. She was more beautiful than ever. Her alabaster complexion was tinted with the touch of a blush and her lips showed the use of a little red brush. Her eyes looked deep ultramarine blue tonight instead of black and they fairly cracked with energy. Her soft brown hair was brushed to a sheen and billowed around her face and shoulders. The only thing missing were the twin dimples.

"Good evening famous man from the east coast. I hope your project is moving along well."

"I'm not talking business, I'm on a winning streak. You want to play some cards or not?"

"My, touchy. You want monte, faro, rouge et noir, Boston, seven up, euchre or maybe some draw poker?"

"Just some twenty-one, less concentration needed."

She smiled. "Why don't you want to concentrate?"

"I knew a beautiful lady gambler once on the Mississippi River boats. She won a pile of money. She figured that she had an advantage. She was an excellent gambler. She could judge other players extremely well, and if all else failed she could flirt so outrageously that the men would lose their concentration."

"And she won?"

"Almost always. She won enough that eventually she bought her own riverboat, married the captain and settled down in St. Louis."

"Shows what can happen to a girl if she isn't careful." They both laughed. Evangeline dealt. Spur was not concentrating. But he never bet more than a dollar on a game, and when he had won fifteen dollars he closed his hands around the cards.

"Enough. Evangeline, you're not concentrating and you sure aren't flirting. What's the matter?"

She watched him for a moment, her dark eyes looking for the smallest hint of how he felt.

"Spur McCoy. I want you to come up to my rooms in back, but I don't know how to ask you. I'm not indicating in any way that I want you to become intimate. But I do want to talk, and to get to know you better, without these damn pasteboards between us."

Spur stood. "I'd be pleased to see you to your door. When we're there you can ask me in, or send me away. That's the time to make the decisions."

She left first, and Spur had one more cold beer at the bar, then went out the front door. He came around to the alley door and she opened it when he knocked. They went up a flight of closed steps to the second floor.

She had moved walls and cut doors and turned the six former cribs into a delightful apartment with kitchen and big sitting room and a large bedroom.

She had not bothered to invite him in, she simply opened the door and walked in and he followed her. She let him light the lamp and she turned up another one and they sat on a sofa in the big room.

"Nice, did you fix it up yourself?"

"Yes." She looked away, then turned back. "Spur McCoy, I'm getting restless. I guess I liked the gambler's life, the moving from town to town. There was always new sights, different kinds of food, fresh faces, vistas and oceans and rivers. Now it's the same day in and day out."

"Take a trip to Europe, you can afford it. Sail across the ocean on one of the steamships."

"Never thought of that. But, no. That doesn't sound good."

"Put in another saloon, make it bigger, fancier."

"Town can't afford one. I would be running a smaller place out of business. I'm not that hungry anymore."

"There's one more route to try."

She looked up, so eager, eyes sparkling, wanting to know.

"What? What else could I try?"

"Take a lover," he said. Spur reached in and let his lips touch hers in a soft, tender kiss.

She pulled back and slapped him.

Spur smiled. He waited, watching her.

Her face twisted into a frown. "Damn, I didn't mean to slap you. Sorry." She moved closer to him, reached up and kissed him. Her arms went around him and the kiss lasted longer than he thought it would.

When she pulled back her eyes came open slowly. Then she caught both of his hands.

"Spur McCoy, I promised myself I wouldn't do that. Damn but I've wanted to. You're such an attractive, such a wonderful man. But that is not saying that I will pretend I'm married to you and jump into bed.

"What I need to do right now is think. You go downstairs and have a beer, and I might come back down. If I don't by the time the beer is gone, my door will be locked and barred."

She pushed toward him again and pressed closely against his chest and kissed him seriously, a lover's kiss. When she pulled away she sighed.

"Oh, glory, but does that bring back memories! Now, Spur McCoy, you be a gentleman and get yourself out of here. On second thought, I'm going to lock and double bar my door as soon as you step out. I've got a lot of thinking to do. And I know that you would not take advantage of me."

Spur bent and kissed the tip of her nose. "You know that a lady never says that unless she is hoping that it will happen." He kissed her lips so softly she barely felt him. But when she opened her eyes he had stood and was near the door.

"Damn, you are leaving."

"When you want me to stay, you'll have the door barred when I'm on the inside," Spur said. He went out the door, down the steps and out the alley to his hotel room.

13

Spur had been in his room at the Aspen Hotel for ten minutes when a soft knock sounded on his door. He had locked it when he came in. He stood at the wash bowl bare to the waist and had just finished scrubbing himself clean.

Spur grabbed his six-gun from his holster hanging on the bed post and moved silently to the door. From the wall beside the opening he paused.

"Yes?" he asked.

"Room service," a woman's voice said.

"What?"

"I've brought up your order from the kitchen," the voice said coming faintly through the panel.

Spur frowned, unlocked the door from the side and holding the pistol ready, swung open the door. Tessie stood there with a covered basket over one arm. She wore a tight blouse, a brown skirt and a big grin.

"Figured it was time I came calling, to welcome a

stranger to our city," she said with a thin smile. Spur remembered her well from the first day he hit town. She was eighteen or a year more, sturdily built with long blonde hair and delicious large breasts. Spur had been in a sexy mood ever since Evangeline had pushed against him in her apartment.

"Can I come in?" Tessie asked. "I've brought you a late night supper, and even a bottle of wine. You like wine?"

Spur chuckled, waved her in and let the hammer down slowly on the Colt. He closed the door and locked it.

"Fact is I am hungry again. What goodies did you bring?"

"Besides me, you mean?" she asked. She put down the basket on the floor and caught his hand and led him to the bed. "First you have to get hungrier." She sat down and he settled beside her.

Her brown eyes glowed with anticipation. Slowly she leaned foward and kissed his lips. Tessie came away slowly. "Oh, yes, yes! You are just as good as I remembered."

Spur unbuttoned the middle of her blouse and pushed his hand inside. There was no other cloth under the blouse and his hand closed around her warm breast.

"Feels so much better when you do that," she said. "I got a sister who's just sixteen and she likes to mess around. We sleep together 'cause we're short on beds. She ain't had a man yet, but some nights we mess around finger fucking each other. She says she likes me better."

"Sixteen? She may change her mind."

"You want to convince her, Spur? You could do it fast."

Spur laughed. "Not if she's sixteen, too young. Give her time." She finished opening the buttons and pulled her blouse off, showing twin mounds, high set with small pink nipples flowering on wide pink areolas.

"If you're really hungry you can chew a while on these," Tessie crooned.

Spur lay on his back and pulled her over him, sucking one breast into his mouth.

"Oh, damn! You know the first time a man did that for me I came right in his face. I mean I exploded and the kid was so surprised he thought he hurt me and ran out of the woods and left me there wanting and with only my own two fingers to push into my burning little pussy. I hope you don't run off and leave me."

Spur changed to her second hanging mound and she groaned in appreciation.

"Oh, yes! Just nothing like a good chew job to get a girl in the mood. Lordy! am I in the mood. I'd guess that you could do me just any way you want to." Her hands stroked his chest, played with the black hair, toyed with his man breast buds.

"Ain't it funny how a woman's tits grow and a man's don't? I wonder why that is? I mean, what good is a man's tits anyway, he don't have no milk. Just kind of a waste."

Spur came away from her and tugged at her skirt. She sat up and stripped off the skirt and wore nothing under it. She pulled at his pants. His boots were already off. When his pants came down he took his underpants with them and she giggled.

"Lordy, I ain't never seen me one any better than

that! Lordy he is big and long and just so delicious!" She dropped on the bed on her hands and knees. "I saw me two dogs just humping up a hurricane today. Do me that way, Spur. I ain't never been done dog fashion before. Bet it is wild!"

Spur hesitated.

"Come on, Spur. I want it that way."

Spur moved up behind her and did what she asked, and only a few seconds later she shrieked.

"Oh, God, I'm gonna explode right now!"

Tessie climaxed three times so quickly that they surged over top of one another, and she lost her balance and fell to the bed. Spur was caught by surprise and before he could stop they both had fallen and rolled off the bed.

Tessie howled in delight as she sprawled beside Spur on the floor. Spur sat up and shook his head.

"That is the most ridiculous thing that ever happened to me in bed with a woman," he said.

Tessie's laughter trailed off and she reached in and kissed Spur, then lifted up on her knees.

"Damn, all this sex makes me hungry. You ready?"

They sat on the bed and examined the wicker basket she had brought. Inside were six drumsticks she had filched from the kitchen, a salt shaker, slabs of bread and fresh butter, half of a lemon cream pie, the wine bottle and two glasses, and six fancily decorated cup cakes.

He reached for the pie.

"That's dessert. Chicken first." She said it with a touch of authority. Then she jerked her head and covered her face with one hand.

"Oops, sorry. I was the oldest of eight. I just naturally had to take care of the little ones."

Spur grabbed a chicken leg, salted it from the shaker and bit into it. To his surprise it was still slightly warm. He made three of the legs vanish and then tried a cup cake.

She watched him, ate nothing herself, and poured the wine. She had no trouble with the cork.

"You like wine?" Tessie asked.

"With good food it goes well sometimes. I'm not one of those people who knows much about the vintages or years or kinds of wine."

"You sure talk fancy. You from back east somewhere? My granddaddy came from Maine."

He told her where he grew up and her eyes widened.

"Really gosh truthful. Is there that many people in one town? A million I heard."

"Could be, I haven't been back there in a few years."

Tessie nodded. "Okay." She reached for Spur's crotch. "Hey, you ever do it while you were eating?"

"What?"

"You know, make love to somebody while you both were eating?"

"No, that would be a first."

"Me too! Let's do it. The pie. We can both be eating the pie and just fucking up a storm!"

Spur laughed, then looked at the pie and fondled her big breasts.

"You are crazy, you know that?"

"Sure, got to be crazy whenever this forest fire gets burning this way between my legs. Only one thing will put out the fire. Come on, let's try!"

She stretched out on the bed holding the half a pie. "You afraid to try it?"

Spur couldn't keep from laughing again. It was so ridiculous it was silly. But he was feeling silly, and as sexy as he ever had.

"A bite of the pie first. I want to be sure it's good." He took the pie from her hand and gouged out a bite, licking his lips when he was done. For an answer he pushed over her and dropped full length on her frame.

Sixty seconds later they were locked together and sharing the pie.

"Bite and stroke," she said and giggled.

By the time the pie was gone, they were both laughing so hard it was difficult to stay sexy. Spur pushed away and sat on the edge of the bed shaking his head.

She stood in front of him putting on her skirt.

"I know just how you feel, Spur McCoy. I was too silly and we lost the serious purpose of sex." Tessie giggled. "But wasn't it a wild party? Can you ever remember having so much fun and laughing so much while you were getting serviced?"

Spur shook his head. "Nothing to compare. You win, hands down." He watched her dress. She came up to him before she buttoned her blouse and let him kiss her breasts goodbye.

"Why do men go crazy over tits? Do you know?"

Spur shook his head.

"I got them with me all the time. Nothing special. But men really get worked up over a tit slipping out of a blouse."

She walked to the door. Tessie had cleaned up the picnic and some of the crumbs. She had the rest of the wine as well.

"Hey, big man. You want a party, you just let me

know. Next one will be totally different. Maybe a drive in the country. You ever made love in the grass?"

She grinned, slipped out the door and closed it.

Spur didn't have any trouble at all going to sleep.

When he woke up the next morning he decided it was time to confront Doc Slocum about the counterfeiting. And he had a good idea how to do it.

After he scrubbed down and shaved, Spur cleaned up the rest of the party from the night before and put on his town clothes, suit pants, a white shirt and string tie and his go-to-meetin' brown doeskin vest. His big six-gun went on his hip tied low.

Spur had a stack of flapjacks and bacon for breakfast, then walked down to Doc Slocum's office and went in. There were two women and a man waiting. He took a chair and a half hour later got in to see the sawbones.

Doc Slocum's cheeks looked pinker this morning, and Spur guessed it was more John Barleycorn than it was sunburn. Doc dropped his 160 pounds into a creaking chair and his brown eyes stared evenly at McCoy.

"Been hearing some strange talk about you, McCoy."

"Do tell. I look strange to you?"

"A mite. Looks don't bother me. Hear you're fancy with that gun of yours, that you know bank robbers and kill them, and that you are something of a poker player."

"Talk does get around."

"You're not here for a medical problem." It was a statement of fact by the doctor.

"That's right. I'm a businessman looking to make a profit."

"I'm just a country doctor . . ."

"That's what most folks hereabouts think. Which is why I'm here. Met a man in Chicago few weeks back. He said you were a good man to know. That you had been in the business before."

Doc scowled, reached in a drawer, then shook his head and shut the drawer. Spur could see the shoulder of a whiskey bottle in the opening.

"Never been to Chicago."

"What he told me. But he said you could help me move some independently produced greenbacks." Doc reacted and Spur hurried on. "Not looking for a big score. You get sixty percent. I've got ten thousand, but I'm willing to give you a thousand worth for just four hundred."

Doc Slocum stared at Spur with anger flashing from his eyes. But his voice was steady when he spoke even though his fingers turned white where his hands gripped the chair.

"Get out of my office! I am not and never have been a counterfeiter. I wouldn't know how to pass your phony bills even if I was tempted. I make a living here, that's all I ask. I even help a few people who are hurting. Now get out of my office."

Spur chuckled and shook his head. "Not a very convincing performance, Doc. The man from Chicago said you'd been away from the trade for a while. Didn't give me a name, but he described you right down to the whiskey cheeks, and brown eyes. He said you were playing at being a doctor here in Johnson Corners."

Doc stood and walked around his desk, stared out the window and then came back and faced Spur.

"I still don't know what you're talking about. I've never been a counterfeiter. I don't want your fake bills. Now please leave. I just heard someone come in who needs me."

"Yeah, right by the script. My friend in Chicago just about called how you would react. He was surprised to know you really was playing doctor, though. The part about the people needing you is good."

Doc Slocum doubled his fists and took a step forward Spur who was still seated, then reconsidered. His face spewed fury.

"My Chicago contact gave me one more persuader. He said I could always go to the local sheriff and ask him to dig up an old wanted poster on you. I think he said the name was Horace Olson. He said you had some major problems in Washington, D.C."

Doc Slocum sat down quickly in his chair. He put his face in his hands for a moment, then recovered. He turned and left the room without another word. Spur followed him but he went to the reception room and asked a lady and a small boy to come into his examining room.

Spur had no chance to push the conversation, or the accusation. Doc would have no hint who Spur was. The friend in Chicago trick must have worked. The more Spur thought about it, the more he was sure that Doc Slocum was not the local funny money maker. If not him, then who could it be?

Spur sat down in the waiting room. A half hour later the woman came out thanking the doctor. The sawbones helped her out the door, then turned and stared at McCoy.

"Come in here, might as well get this over with."

He walked into his office where they had talked before.

When they both sat down, Doc Slocum leaned over his desk.

"Now, let's get it out in the open. What's this about counterfeit money?"

Spur took out four of the five dollar bills with identical serial numbers and laid them side by side on the desk.

"Check the serial numbers. They are about as phony as they get."

Doc looked at them and shrugged. "If you say so. I wouldn't know one from the other. But I do know that each bill is supposed to have a different number. So they are fake, I don't know anything about them."

"Is that the truth, Doc?"

"Damn right! I don't like . . ." He sighed. "All right. I never expected to be able to hide this long. You're right, my real name is Horace Olson, and I came from Washington, D.C. But that was a long time ago. I made a small mistake and I paid a terrible price for it."

"Small mistake? Counterfeiting and murder are not exactly small mistakes."

"Murder? Not me, I was never . . ."

"You were charged by the Washington police with murder and counterfeiting."

"No! If it was Archibald Vincent you're talking about who died, he had a bad heart. I kept warning him. Then one day he got excited and his heart simply gave out on him. That was at the same time the counterfeiting scheme he headed went bad and I ran as far and as fast as I could."

"So you knew about the counterfeiting?"

"Not until the last few days. They used some of my offices, and my people. They even forged my name on some orders. I was the legitimate front for them and they took advantage of me. I knew nothing about the making of fake bills."

Spur watched him. Doc had an honest face. Spur had been watching men try to lie out of problems for years now and he had an uncanny nack for picking out the liars from those telling the truth.

"There's still a warrant out for you in Washington, D.C., Doc. What are we going to do about that?"

Doc's pudgy, pink face reddened even more. Sweat beaded on his forehead.

"Christ, I don't know, McCoy. I've battled this for a long time. Didn't do a damn thing wrong, but knew I'd get burned for it. I should have stayed and cleared it up. Too damn late now. Guess you'll have to decide. But if you arrest me, I'll get a lawyer and fight it from here. You'll have a battle on your hands."

Spur stood up. "Yep, reckoned that I might. I better talk to some more folks around town before I decide. Oh, that counterfeiting here in Johnson Corners. Keep that quiet for now, all right? I want to surprise the culprit."

"Fine by me." Doc stood. "Just remember, the folks in this town got only one doctor. They won't take kindly to losing him, even if it's just me."

14

On the way back toward his hotel from Doc Slocum's office, Spur passed Priscilla Davis's store. She stood at the open front door and motioned for him to come in. He turned on the boardwalk and moved to the screen door which she held open.

"I really need to talk to you for a few minutes, Mr. McCoy," she said formally. He nodded and went inside. No one else seemed to be in the store.

She caught his hand and led him behind the cash register where the back room started and they were shielded from the street. Impulsively she reached up and kissed him, pressing her body firmly against his from crotch to chest and Spur felt the instant heat of her flesh.

"Oh, my, that is nice," Priscilla said. She stepped back. "I know we can't stretch out here on the floor right now, but I desperately wanted to kiss you again." She frowned. "Actually I needed to kiss you and tell you what I've decided. I think it's time the store has a man to help fun it. Some of the things I don't know much about. Oh, I can get along, but it takes a man's touch.''

She watched him closely.

"Spur, I'm offering to sell you half the store for a thousand dollars. Then if things work out right, I want to marry you and turn the whole thing over to you and have six babies with you as their father. Spur, my own true love, I want to have a baby so bad!''

"Priscilla, that just wouldn't work out. My job keeps me moving around a lot. I'm just not ready to settle down to any one town.''

"But you could be ready if I helped." She opened her blouse and spread it to show her breasts. Priscilla walked up to him and took his hands and put them on her chest. Then she stroked his crotch and found Spur's stiffening penis.

"See! See! He wants to stay with me! He wants to come inside me right now. I know he does!''

Spur fondled her breasts a moment, then stepped back.

"Priscilla, I never told you I loved you or wanted to stay here. I can't. I have to move on. There is just no chance that we could be married, so forget about that. You told me you just wanted to have a good time.''

"No! I always wanted to marry you. I demonstrated that the first time when you attacked me and raped me. I didn't complain. Then in your room I didn't scream when you forced yourself on me again.''

Her face clouded and anger sparked from her eyes. "But now, now, Spur McCoy, you are trifling with my affection. You have ruined me, made love to me, maybe even made me pregnant! You will marry me in case I might get pregnant, or I'll get the sheriff after you. I'll charge you with rape, three times, with raping me and now leaving me.''

"That's not what happened, Priscilla. I didn't rape you. The whole sexy meeting was your idea, you insisted, you led. If anything, you were the one who seduced me that first time, as you very well know.''

Fury built in her. She charged at him, her blouse still open, her breasts bouncing as she tried to scratch his face. He caught her hands.

"Not a chance in hell, woman!" Spur said softly. "You go ahead and play your games, but with somebody else. When you do get pregnant you'll have to move to another town or try to figure out who got you in a family way.''

He threw her hands down and she slumped against the wall.

"Now forget it. The sheriff probably already knows about your open blouse policy, how you throw yourself at men. From now on we'll just steer clear of each other!''

"No! I'll die if you don't marry me!''

Spur laughed. "You must have been an actress, but this performance isn't that good. For your own good, just stay away from me.''

Spur marched back to the front door, turned and scowled at Priscilla who still hadn't closed her blouse. He shrugged and went out the door to the boardwalk.

He was about to step off the walk into the street when he saw a gray horse coming toward him.

Astride the mount sat Willard Kleaner.

Spur waved at him and Willard pulled the gray to a stop next to Spur.

"Seen my new horse yet, Mr. McCoy?" Willard asked, his eyes glowing with pride.

"Not close up, Willard. A fine a looking gray as I've seen in a long time. Is she yours?"

"Yes sir. Bought her with my own money. Now I need to learn how to ride better and to rope. Can you . . ." Willard hesitated. "Mr. McCoy, can you use a rope?"

"Tolerable, Willard. I've earned my keep on a cattle drive or two."

"Could you teach me? I got a rope along with my outfit."

"Right now?"

"Why not? I got time before I got to work."

Spur put his hands on his hips and frowned at the boy. Then he grinned. "A half hour, if you'll practice tonight for an hour."

Willard promised that he'd practice and they went down the alley until they came to a fence and Spur took the lariat. It was a good cowboy's rope. He set a loop and swung it around his head once and pitched the open hoop over a fence post and snaked the rope tight.

"Easy once you get the hang of it," Spur explained. "The important thing is to keep your loop open so it can catch what you're throwing at. You ever see a roundup or a branding on one of the ranches round here?"

"Golly, no, Mr. McCoy."

"Should ride out to a ranch and watch one some time. Do you good. When they brand range cattle one cowboy ropes the front two legs of the steer, then the other man ropes the back two. That's the hard part. First you just learn how to catch that fence post."

Spur showed him how to hold the rope, how to set the loop and hold it, then swing it around his head. The first time Willard threw the rope he forgot to hold on to the loose end. By the fifth throw Willard roped the fence post.

"It's harder to do when you're on a horse because you're at a different angle and you're moving, but then so might be your target. You learn to rope the posts for a while. That'll keep you busy."

Willard moved forward and back, and then began walking past the post. On almost every turn he caught the post. At the end of fifteen minutes Spur held up his hands.

"Enough for one day. Didn't you say you had to get to the hotel to work?"

"Yeah. Wish I didn't." His young jaw set in a hard line. "One of these days I'll get good enough with my rope and horse so I can go get a job on a ranch as a real cowboy."

Not a lot of that work up this high in the mountains," Spur said. "But you keep working at it."

Willard took something from his saddlebag and brought it over to Spur.

"Look what I got me just today!" Willard said with a bucket just running over with pride.

He unwrapped an old, and well worn .44 six-gun.

Spur looked at it with surprise. He picked it up, hefted it, tried the action and spun the cylinder. It was empty. Most of the bluing had worn off it. One walnut hand grip was missing. Spur handed the weapon back holding the barrel.

"No need for you to get a six-gun," Spur said. "I

kind of wish you hadn't. Most cowboys wear six-guns only to shoot at rattlesnakes. Most of them miss.''

"But all the cowboy books say that every range hand has a six-gun and a rifle and can use them!''

"Dime store novels don't picture the West how it really is, Willard. They write how they think it is. Most of those writers never ventured west of the Mississippi river.''

Willard looked shocked. He wrapped up the weapon in a greasy cloth and stared at Spur.

"Mr. McCoy, I can't rightly believe that. I don't aim to get no bullets for it. Not yet.''

"Willard, keep it wrapped up in the barn somewhere. Don't take it out on the street. A piece like that could get you in big trouble. You understand?''

"Yes, I understand, Mr. McCoy. I promise to keep it put away, for a while at least.''

They walked back to the hotel and Willard tied his gray to the hitching rail in front of the hostelry and stared up the steps.

Ronald Lewton, the hotel owner, stood on the top step waiting for him.

Spur walked up with Willard and watched Lewton. The smaller man nodded at Spur then turned to Willard.

"You're ten minutes late. What are you trying to do, make me angry? You know what your responsibilities are.'

"Yes sir. I was just . . .'' He stopped. "I won't be late again, I promise.'' He hurried into the hotel.

Spur stared hard at Lewton.

"Kind of hard on the boy, aren't you?''

"That's my business, sir. No, I don't want to sell my hotel. That completes our business.''

Spur shook his head. "Not really, Lewton. I hear the boy has quite an inheritance coming to him. You keep treating him this way and he'll hate you by the time he gets his money. Is that what you want?"

Lewton jerked his head back in surprise. "No, no of course not. I'm just trying to do what's best for Willard. Lost both his parents."

"I heard. Also understand there's twenty dollars a month that you get to help raise the boy."

Lewton stiffened. "Which is absolutely no business of yours, sir!"

"You're right. But it might be some interest to the boy. Best you think about that sometime. Relax a little. He's a good kid, and he's going to be a man in two or three years."

Lewton turned and stalked into the hotel without looking back. Spur shrugged. He had tried. He'd seen it happen before. Spur walked down the steps to the first set of chairs outside the front of a store and sat in one and leaned back against the wall. He tilted his hat down over his eyes and put his mind to work on the problem.

Point one: Doc Slocum probably wasn't guilty of anything more than choosing the wrong friends in Washington, D.C. But Spur still had to take him in —or come up with some mighty convincing evidence for his superiors.

Point two: He still had a counterfeiter at large in the small village he had to find. He was near certain now that the man was not Doc Slocum. The sawbones had been totally surprised by the evidence Spur had shown him.

So who? One of the bigger gambling palaces? They could finance their whole operation that way, lose for a while and then win it all back with a big stack of chips bought with bogus money.

The only trouble with that theory was that Evangeline's was the biggest, richest saloon-gaming house in town. He'd lay high odds that Evangeline was not the fake money producer. She wasn't the type.

So who did he have left? Just a few merchants who seemed to be scratching to pay the rent or the mortgage to the bank every month.

The newsman? Highly unlikely. His establishment was not flush with money. The very nature of most newsmen was honesty to the core.

Spur went over the alternatives again in his mind, then dropped the front legs of the chair to the boardwalk with a thumb and stood. He knew where he might find some answers. There was one place, and one person in the average small Western town where the most was known about the area and its people. He hoped that Johnson Corners had a good reliable representative of the profession.

Spur grinned and turned up the street in the direction of the Palace, Johnson Corners' only whorehouse.

15

The only fancy lady house in town was a former residence a block off Main Street just one street down from the bank. It was fancy, with gingerbread work around the windows, cupolas, big windows on all three floors, and three chimneys for the fireplaces.

Spur had heard about Princess Hanshoe the first day he was in town. She ran the local house and the sheriff made sure she had no competition as long as she kept the price reasonable, the girls as clean as possible and at least one who was somewhat pretty.

Spur started to knock, but a small neatly painted sign on the door said: "You made it this far, Come On IN!"

He turned a silver knob and let himself in. It was an entrance hall, the kind many homes in the East had where you could take off heavy wraps, and put down umbrellas and overshoes.

A small bell rang when he opened the door. Now

he heard a mumble of voices from somewhere in the house.

"It's only ten-thirty in the morning for god's sake!" one piercing voice protested.

Spur grinned. The ladies must have had a long night of work. As he waited he looked at the decorations. There were oil paintings on three of the four walls, two of them quite good showing a seascape in one and a landscape in the other. Both were unsigned.

He was admiring the brush work on the seascape when footsteps sounded behind him. He did not turn.

"Fascinated by the delicate work on that one?" a husky voice asked behind him. It was female but just barely.

"As a matter of fact I am," Spur said. "It's good. There's no signature. Is it a local artist?" He turned and smiled down at a short, slightly plump woman in her forties. She wore a bathrobe and had a kerchief hiding her hair.

The woman looked as if she had just woke up. Large blue eyes stared out at him from a slightly puffy face that had no other color at all. She frowned.

"Damn right it's by a local artist, me. I used to know how to do that." She squinted at him. "Oh, yeah. You're the new man in town. Trying to buy a business, you wanted us to think. Most figure you're some kind of a lawman, that is after the way you brought in them two bank robbers. Thanks for saving my money in the bank."

Spur grinned. "You're welcome. Spur McCoy is the name, and you're right. I don't want to buy your house."

"Damn, probably the only chance I'll ever have. You ain't here to get serviced, that's for damn certain. Good looker like you won't never have to pay for love."

"Just need to talk. You had your morning coffee yet?"

She laughed. "You can call me Princess. Fact is I ain't had coffee nor the potty or nothing yet. Usual we don't get woke up this time of day."

"I'll make the fire if you'll get the coffee pot," Spur said.

"Damn, didn't think they made them like you any more. Follow me to the coffee pot."

She led the way to the kitchen where Spur got the fire going from cut kindling and branches, then added some split fir and soon the fire heated through the iron grate and into the coffee water. They sat at a cheerful kitchen table and looked out on a back yard that sported a fence to fence garden that already had rows of growing vegetables.

"What I hate most about this country is the short growing season. Now down in Tennessee we had a season that lasts three times as long as we have here."

"You have a good knack with a garden."

"Like to try. You said you wanted to talk."

Spur told her about the phony money, laid out the four five dollar bills.

"Figured you was the law, never guessed from Washington, D.C. Wow." She put in the coffee and let it boil. "No sir, them bills would fool me. Probably got some now with that same serial number. What do I do with them?"

"Keep them, for now. My job is to find out who is running his own printing press."

"Somebody here in town?"

"Probably. At least someone here must be passing the money. Who would have that chance? Who could do it?" He paused while she frowned, thinking. "There could even be a hint, a bit of talk in the heat of passion, bragging by some man who wanted to impress a lady . . ."

"Not a chance. Professional secrets."

"This counterfeiter could ruin the town. If word gets out it could make people accept only gold coins. Cause one hell of a mess. You wouldn't want that to happen, Princess."

"And you could get nasty about my business, I know. Well, let me think."

She stood, moved to the stove and slid the coffee back off the heat to let it settle, then poured two cups and provided Spur with sugar and milk, but he used neither.

"I'm thinking, don't rush me."

A door to one side opened and a girl walked in. She wore a man's pants cut off at the knees and nothing else. Her long red hair was mussed, her face still sleepy. She had large breasts, heavily nippled, that swayed as she walked. She saw Spur and stopped for a moment.

Then she shrugged, went to the stove and poured a cup of coffee and without a word sat down at the table across from Spur. She didn't say a thing, simply drank her coffee and stared at Spur.

Princess began to nod. "Yeah, something is coming. Somebody said something about having a way to get rich, but he wasn't going to. Instead he was going to help the whole town. Said he had a regular money machine."

Spur tried to concentrate on Princess but his gaze

kept wandering back to the girl's breasts. She was smiling at him now waking up gradually. She moved and her breasts bounced.

"Vivian, stop that! He's not a customer."

"Might be if I shake them just right. I wouldn't mind, right now. Right here on the table. Hell, I'll give him a pop for free. Ain't he pretty?"

Princess shook her head. "It's hard as hell to get good help these days, Spur. This one for instance. Good tits, but no sense of business."

Spur laughed and looked back at Princess. "That sounds like my man, the one who wanted to help the whole town. Can you remember who he was?"

Princess shook her head. "He was drunk at the time, and I just ignored what he said. Lots of men get a little drunk and before they come. I can't remember who he was. A regular. I usually don't work, but we were really busy that night."

"Sounds like the newspaper guy," Vivian said.

"No, not him. He don't come in much." Princess shook her head and then closed her eyes thinking.

Vivian cupped her breasts and lifted them for Spur's benefit, then stood and leaned over making them swing down showing their true size.

"Vivian, get another cup of coffee and get your big tits out of here," Princess said. "I'm trying to think."

Vivian grinned, leaned in and kissed Spur on the cheek, then filled her coffee cup and swayed out the door.

Princess shook her head. "No use. I can't think of his name right now. But I will. Might take me some time. Where you staying? I'll send a note to you when I get the name." Spur told her. She stood up.

"Now to more interesting things." Princess

grinned. "One nice thing about this business. Your basic stock is always there and it don't wear out or get used up. You want Vivian? A free one to show my appreciation to the folks in Washington."

Spur stood and shook his head. "She's not really my type, Princess. And right now I'm on duty, so I can't. You understand."

"Sure, if she don't get you a hard-on, she don't. The matter is closed. I'll come up with the name in a day or two. Damn sure I will. Got me a good memory."

"Just one caution, Princess. What we talked about can't leave this room. It has to be in the strictest confidence. I need to surprise the counterfeiter. If he gets wind I'm here on his trail, he'll vanish or destroy the evidence and I'll never get this worked out."

"You bet. I don't tell tales out of school."

Spur finished his coffee, thanked the madam and went out the front door. Two spinster types met him on the sidewalk and sniffed self righteously as they passed him.

Spur was tempted to ask them if they lived at the house, but merely chuckled to himself and went down to Main Street.

Spur walked back to his hotel room where he washed up and changed his shirt, then had an early noon meal in the hotel dining room. He winked at Tessie in the hallway. She motioned him into the room she was cleaning, but he grinned and walked the other way.

He got to Doc Slocum's office just before he closed for dinner. There was only one other patient in the waiting room when Spur arrived and the medico took care of her quickly. He let her out and locked the outer door, then stared at Spur.

"I suppose you're here to argue with me."

"Not at all. But we do need to talk. I've got this warrant with both your names on it, and a boss in Washington who is hounding me to bring your body back to the capital for a trial. What the hell am I supposed to do?"

Doc Slocum sat on the white painted wooden bench along one wall of the waiting room and rubbed his face with his hands. His fat cheeks looked redder today.

"I had studied two years to be a doctor in Washington before I ran out of money and had to quit, did you know that? Then I got into business but I never got back to medicine. When everything blew up I left my wife and baby girl and ran. Yes, I'm a coward, too.

"I wasn't strong enough to face the public scandal, even though I knew I'd win. It was too much for me."

"So you came West."

"To a small town where they didn't have a doctor. I still had all my medical books, and I got some more. I put in six hours every night after my office closed for two years going through the last of the medical learning I needed. So nobody can say I'm not a trained physician. That much about me is honest and straight."

"Requirements for physicians are not really set up yet here," Spur said. "We have no argument with you on that score."

"You know I'm the only doctor for thirty, thirty-five mile ride in any direction? What these folks going to do for a doctor if you haul me out of here?"

"Worries me a lot, Doc. Convince me you should stay."

"Told you, Archibald Vincent died of a heart

attack. He wasn't shot or stabbed or strangled. How did the police say he died?"

"They didn't. My report just says he was killed."

"So straighten them out on it. He died a natural death, and nobody is a murderer. I laid it out for you about the counterfeiting. They used me. They used my small firm and my connection with the printing company and did things in my name I never authorized. I was duped."

"Might be hard to prove now one way or another," Spur said with a long puzzled look.

"McCoy, you'd be wasting tax payers money to haul me back to the capital for a trial. I'll get a good lawyer and he can prove in a minute that I'm not guilty of anything. You won't even be able to bring charges before they're thrown out of court. I know that much about the law."

"I'm starting to agree with you. Let me think it over. You can help your case by helping me on this other problem, the local counterfeiting."

"I told you, I wouldn't know how to start."

"But you know this town. Who in town is smart enough and has enough connections in Denver, probably, to get plates made and print off all this fake money?"

"Sure it's here in town?"

"No, but it's a good bet. Who could do it?"

"Take some thinking. I could come up with two or three right off. We have a lawyer by the name of Nevin Nelson. He's smart enough. He has a good practice, could float a lot of fake money. And he goes to Denver once a month at least. Has some clients there I understand."

"Sounds promising. Who else?"

"Josh, the livery man. He might not look it, but

he's the second richest man in town next to our banker. He owns about half of Main Street. Bought the land early, and put up the stores as he had money and kept renting them. He don't have to work if he don't want to. Likes to keep his hand in. Reckon he could hire somebody to do the Denver part. Trouble is, Josh has more money now than he can ever spend. Why would he make fake money? It just doesn't figure."

"Good point. But for some men, there never is enough money. Maybe Josh wants to own all of the town, including the bank. How well do you know him?"

"Not a chance he could do that. Those are the only two names I can come up with right off. Let me do some thinking." He watched Spur.

"Are you satisfied that I have nothing to do with the counterfeiting here in town?"

"Coming around that way. You don't take in enough cold cash to pass more than about fifty dollars a year." Spur paused. "Oh, Doc, you ever remarry?"

"Course not, I'm still married. Can't get me on that one. I do have a woman. We pretended to get married. Living in sin, but I'm no bigamist. And yes, I send money to my wife every month. She must know it comes from me. I send it through a Denver bank so my name or address is never used."

"I'm sorry about all this, Doc."

"Yeah, you look just sorry as hell. Now I need to get something to eat before folks start coming in again. You mind if I go have some dinner?"

Spur stood and walked to the door, unlatched it and looked back. "Doc, we nail down that counterfeiter, then we'll decide just what to do about you, fair enough? It's going to take some tall convincing.''

"I could hire somebody to gun you down in some alley, McCoy," Doc said.

"Could, Doc, but you won't. I've seen too many killers. You just aren't one of them." Spur turned his back on the doctor and offered his back as a target as he walked out the door, closing it softly behind him.

16

Spur left the medical offices and walked two blocks back toward the center of the small town. He was not sure what to do about the doctor. It might take a couple of days to sort it all out. From the vague nature of his orders, he realized now there was some confusion in Washington about the case as well.

He slowed as he passed the alley next to the saddle shop. As he did a six-gun thundered from the narrow space and Spur felt a rush of air as a bullet slammed past his chest and dug into the street beyond him.

Spur lunged forward out of the alley and to the boardwalk next to the saddle shop, and drew his own weapon as he peered around the corner. Another slug tore into the wood just over his head and he jerked back out of sight.

For a fleeting moment he wondered if he had misjudged Doc Slocum. Then he shook his head. Impossible. The medic just wasn't the killing type. He bellied down on the boardwalk and peeked around the corner of the store from ground level. All he saw was a shadowy figure vanishing around the far end of the alley into the next street.

Spur leaped up and raced down the alley, paused at the end of it and looked out into the street. There were only two businesses here and a pair of houses. A man sat on a horse across the street watching Spur.

The man walked the mount across and grinned. "Guess you're after that person who came out of the alley just a minute ago. She was running right scared. Didn't get a good look at her but she had on a dark blue dress and a blue bonnet. She went into that second store down there, the feed store."

"A woman?"

"Right sure of that, mister. Pretty one, too."

Spur thanked him and walked quickly to the Corners Feed Store and went inside.

At once he was assaulted by the meal-like smell of crushed oats, ground corn and cracked wheat. The store front was backed by a small elevator and a feed grinding mill.

There was no one in the store. Spur went through the open door in back into the mill section. A man stood sacking grain from a hopper. He looked up and waved. The falling grain made so much noise speaking was of little use.

Spur looked around the milling area quickly and found the woman in a blue dress and blue bonnet standing behind sacks of grain.

"Well, Priscilla Davis. I should have known. I'm glad you're not a better shot." This far from the hopper they could talk and be understood.

She frowned, drew back. "I don't know what

you're talking about. I came in here for feed for my horse."

"Of course you did. But that was after you took two shots at me up on Main Street."

Spur moved quickly, jerked her reticule from her hands and opened it. Inside he found a weapon. He pulled it out and sniffed the barrel. It had been fired recently. He looked at it closer. It was a .38 caliber center fire weapon made only the year before, a Remington New Line Revolver #3. It was light with no trigger guard but used a rod ejector. A woman's gun.

He pushed the weapon in his belt and led her back into the store and then outside to the dusty street.

"I should take you down to the sheriff and charge you with attempted murder."

"You can't prove anything, Spur McCoy. Lots of people want to shoot you. I've heard you're here to take our doctor away. A lot of the woman are talking about it. They plan on stopping you. If I shot at you, I had a much better reason than that."

"You did try to kill me. Why?"

"Because you're supposed to marry me, and now you're backing out of it. I hate you!"

"Probably, but that's all your own doing. You better just forget about me and run your store, and find some nice quiet way to trap a man into marrying you. For you, getting pregnant might be the best idea after all."

Priscilla shouted something at him in fury and marched away through the inch-deep dust of the street toward her store.

Spur watched her go. She would be more trouble for him, he knew. The woman was not at all stable. He was surprised she had survived this long. There was a type of man who would love to move in on her, marry her, loot the store and house and ride off with the profits. So far she had been lucky.

Spur touched the long barreled Colt in his holster and walked toward the newspaper office. He had been headed there when Priscilla bushwhacked him. He wanted to lay his cards on the table for the newsman and see what help he could be. Spur was near-certain now that Hans Walker was not the counterfeiter.

However, Walker could be a good source of information about who the counterfeiter might be.

When Spur walked in the shop, Hans had his editor's hat on. He was furiously working at the front desk writing with a stub pencil on a pad of paper.

"Sorry, can't talk now, have to get this story done so it can be in this week's edition."

"You publish every week?"

"Well, no. Usually we wait until we have enough news and enough ads to make it worth while. You a newsman?"

"No. I'm a lawman, and I want to give you the biggest story you've ever had."

"The bank robbery is the one, I bet. Tell me how you knew about it going to happen. Is it true that you knew that dead man before, what was his name?"

"Abe Varner. Yes, I knew him before. Chased him before."

"Figured from what the sheriff said."

"I don't want to talk about the robbery. I want to talk about these." Spur handed the newspaperman the four five dollar bills."

"Is that genuine U.S. currency?"

Hans turned the bills over, felt of them, then nodded. "Sure seem good to me. Course I don't handle that much money every day. Our banker would know."

"He didn't. Check them again."

"Well, if you're so keen on them, at least one of them must be a bad bill, but I swear I can't tell which one."

"Look at the serial numbers."

"Land sakes! They all have the same number. So they all are counterfeit?"

"Right. My job is to find out who made and passed them."

"And since I have a printing press, I'm a suspect?"

"No. I've ruled you out. Not much goes on here nights, and you were surprised by the fake bills. Besides, you have no good way to pass the money."

"So you're giving me a story about the counterfeiting?"

"No, this is all confidential. What I want from you is help. Some suggestions about who in town might be prone to this sort of scheme and would have the contacts to do it."

"My first choice would be our banker, Bart Concord. But if you know him the idea is ludicrous. He isn't living high, he doesn't go to Denver every week to spend his money. His house is no better than mine and he dresses like everyone else. If he did it he didn't make a cent from the operation.

"So I'd have to go on to our bigshot lawyer who moved here from Denver after some family scandal."

"That would be Nevin Nelson?"

"Exactly. Never could find out what happened in

Denver, but the rumor is that he got his sister-in-law pregnant. Her husband, his brother, was sterile, and suddenly she starts to get a swelled belly, and all hell broke loose. Word is that he'd been bedding her for two years."

"So he'd have the connections for an engraver and printer in Denver and the morals to do the job?"

"About what I'm saying, McCoy. When can I print the story?"

"When I arrest someone. Not a word before, otherwise the culprit will take off scotfree."

"Understood. Not let me fill in some blanks I have on this robbery story. You killed Varner while he was threatening others in the bank. How many shots did you fire?"

"One."

Spur spent another fifteen minutes answering questions for the newsman, then thanked him and went out to the boardwalk. It took him five minutes to find the lawyer's office. It was upstairs over the barbershop. Spur knocked on the outer door and went in.

The office was well furnished, better than most of the houses in town, Spur decided. Carefully crafted oak furniture, some with thick upholstery, filled the room. A large oak desk sat in one corner and behind it a tall, broad shouldered man sat with a thin cigar in a long holder. He looked up, curious.

"Yes?"

"Mr. Nelson?"

"Yes. How can I help you?"

"I need some professional advice about a piece of property. I'm willing to pay."

"I charge two dollars an hour."

"That much? A working man earns little more

than a dollar a day, maybe thirty dollars a month."

"My fee is two dollars an hour for professional advice."

Spur shrugged. "All right. I want to know what the legal status is of the store owned and run by Priscilla Davies. Also about what the market value of the store is and if the building and land go with it."

"She wants to sell?" Nelson asked.

"That's not what I'm paying you for. I want to know the legal status of the property and business."

"Yes, of course. I can have that information for you by tomorrow."

Spur had not sat down. He took a twenty dollar double gold eagle from his pocket and handed it to the lawyer. "I prefer to pay in advance, will four dollars cover the bill?"

"Probably." The lawyer took out a purse and extracted a single and three five dollar bills. He gave them to Spur who folded them and put them in his pocket.

"I'll be by at noon tomorrow for the information. I just hope you have the answers I want." He walked out without saying goodbye.

Down the steps, Spur leaned against the wall and examined the five dollar bills. All the serial numbers were different, all had numbers not on the counterfeit bills. At least the lawyer wasn't passing them brazenly himself. It meant nothing. Spur had to find out more about this lawyer.

Spur turned back toward the Aspen Hotel. It was hot and he wanted a bath before dinner. He didn't care if Tessie came and scrubbed his back or not. He felt grimy.

He was half a block away from the hotel when he

saw a commotion in front of the hostelry. Two dozen women were milling about. Most of them had children in tow. They completely blocked the steps up to the hotel.

He frowned and continued forward out of curiosity. Something had the women all excited. It could be the vote. They didn't have it here yet.

He was at the edge of the group of women angling for the side of the steps when one of the women shouted.

"That's him! That's Spur McCoy, the federal lawman who wants to steal our doctor away from us!"

The women pushed their children ahead of them, held hands with the other women and before he knew it, had circled him and trapped him in their midst.

"You can't take our doctor away!" one woman shouted.

"I have four children who need Doc Slocum. You take him away and you kill one of my children!"

Spur held up his hands but they kept shouting. They hit the same theme over and over again. When Spur tried to push through the circle, two small boys grabbed his legs and hung on. The women shoved him back into the circle.

At last all of them quieted but one, who seemed to be the spokesman. She moved inside the circle and stared at Spur.

"Mr. McCoy. We realize that you are a federal lawman and that you've come to town for a purpose. We know you have a duty to do here. All we want to do is consider all the facts. We don't believe that Doctor George Slocum committed any foul deed in the East.

"Further we believe that even if he had, the good

works, the humanitarian efforts, the Christian charity the man has shown since he's been our doctor here, overbalance by a hundred fold any misdemeanor he may have committed.

"Without Doc Slocum this town would be in continual danger. There is no doctor for thirty-five to forty miles in any direction. We are isolated here and need a resident medical expert.

"Will you agree to let our doctor stay in town?"

The women were quiet. A horse whinnied down the street. Somewhere a leather whip cracked over the back of a stubborn mule.

"Ladies, I share your concern for Johnson Corners. I am still gathering evidence. What you have to say will have a bearing on whether Doc Slocum stays or leaves this community. However this is a matter for the law, not for a mob. Violence and mob action will not be tolerated. I have jurisdiction here and anyone who participates in a mob will be punished, whether that person is a man or a woman."

"Let us keep our doctor! He saved my baby's life when he was only three weeks old!" someone shouted.

"Without him this town could dry up and be eaten by the squirrels. Save our doctor!"

"Temper your justice with some mercy!" another shrilled.

"Save our doctor!" someone screamed.

The group picked it up as a chant and repeated it over and over again. Wagons stopped in the street. Riders reined in and soon the street in front of the hotel was clogged with buggies, wagons and the stage coach which came rolling in.

Spur edged toward the ring of women. They held

fast. He caught the wrists of two women in his powerful hands.

"I'm going to pull your hands apart. I don't want to hurt you. Why don't you just let go by yourself?"

Neither woman would look at him and held on tightly. Spur tugged a moment, then pulled harder and their hands came apart. He hurried up the steps and into the hotel before the women could stop him.

He continued upstairs to his outside room and watched from behind the closed curtains. The women remained in the street and on the steps for an hour. Spur did not get a bath, and he was late getting down to supper that evening. He was sure of one thing. If Doc Slocum did stay in Johnson Corners he would be more appreciated than ever. Now all Secret Agent Spur had to do was decide whether to take Doc Slocum back for trial or not.

17

That evening Spur wandered into the Evangeline Saloon and Gaming House and played some faro but lost twenty dollars quickly and gave it up. He saw Evangeline supervising the whole operation from her raised table and walked over to her.

"Just the man I want to see," she said sternly. "You have some explaining to do. I hear that you were serenaded tonight by some of our unhappy women."

"True, are you going to join the chorus?"

"I sing only solo . . . or perhaps sometimes in duet."

Spur slumped in the chair. "I've got a hell of a problem. Any suggestions?"

"Not a one. Out of my area of concern." She brightened and both dimples popped inward. "Want to play some twenty-one?"

"Not really. I'm on a losing streak."

"How about some poker, that's the thinking man's game."

Spur wrinkled his brow and shook his head slowly. "Too many distractions down here."

He watched her. She looked up and saw him. Her dimples vanished, her smile faded. For a moment she was totally serious.

"Do you want to come upstairs and play?"

He touched her hand and was surprised when she jumped.

"Yes, Evangeline. I would like to come upstairs with you."

"And play poker," she added quickly.

"Yes, and play poker."

He left first, went out the front door and waited ten minutes, then went around to the saloon's private back door. It was unlocked. He went in, locked it behind him and walked quietly up the steep wooden stairs to the apartment over the saloon.

She met him at the door, stood on tip toes and kissed his lips quickly, then scurried away.

"Coffee, tea, wine or whiskey?"

"Coffee is too much trouble. How about a light whiskey and branch water."

"Make that two," she said softly and smiled at his surprise. "Remember a good gambler has to be able to hold her whiskey. I lost a big game only once because I couldn't drink as much as the men in the game. Never happened again."

They sat at a small table and she brought out the whiskey bottle, two glasses and a pitcher of cold water.

"All the comforts of the bar," he said.

She let him fix the drinks as she dealt a hand of

five card draw poker. They had no chips. There was no talk of any stakes.

They played two games and were on their second whiskey when she frowned.

"McCoy, there is no incentive to play well, to win. We need some stakes."

"Chips, matches, double eagles?"

She shook her head. She bent in and kissed him again and let her lips linger on his. Evangeline sighed, and watched him from so close she couldn't focus on his face. She edged back until he cleared and she smiled.

"Mr. McCoy. This is going to take some doing, and some getting used to for me, but I have decided that I am going to seduce you before the night is over. But that means I'm going to need some encouragement, some incentive."

Evangeline giggled and Spur saw the whiskey at work.

"Which means I think we should play strip poker!"

Spur laughed softly, reached in and kissed her cheek, then her lips quickly. "Good idea. Body stakes, whatever we're wearing is all we can bet."

She nodded and dealt a hand of seven card stud. It took more betting.

"A shoe to ante," Evangeline said. She slid off one of her shoes and put it on the table. Spur bent and unlaced his boot, then pulled it off and put it beside the shoe.

Spur won with a full house, Aces up.

A half hour later, Spur won a pot of two shoes, two socks, a blouse and a shirt.

'House rule," Evangeline said. "Once . . . once a

person takes off an item of clothing, it can't be put back on."

Spur nodded. He sat wearing only his pants. She had on a skirt and her chemise which covered her but outlined clearly her thrusting breasts.

The next hand was draw poker. Spur had most of the clothes they had taken off. Evangeline had only what she wore and two socks.

The game was seven card stud and Spur dealt. She bet a sock each time as the second and third cards came face up. Spur was high with a pair of deuces and he bet a sock.

Evangeline motioned to him. "Kiss me," she said softly. He leaned in and kissed her lips and was surprised how they fluttered open for a moment, then closed. When they parted she lifted the chemise over her head and put it in the pot.

Her breasts were small and firm, with bright red nipples over nearly colorless areolas.

"Beautiful!" Spur whispered.

"Then kiss me and then them," Evangeline said.

When he kissed her, her mouth was open and she stood slowly and broke off the kiss and led him toward the bedroom.

"I'm tired of playing cards," she said with a sly smile. "Can you think of any other game we could play?"

"I'll do my best," Spur said.

They settled down on the edge of the bed and she reached for his pants and quickly unbuttoned the fly.

"I want to see the good stuff!" she said. She pulled down his pants and short underwear together until his erection slanted upward.

"Oh, sweet mother, look at that!" She turned to

him and took a deep breath. "He's so beautiful you should never hide him!" She pulled his pants off the rest of the way and threw them on the floor. Then she pushed to the middle of the bed.

"You haven't kissed my bouncers yet."

Spur did, working around each breast, capping the journey by kissing, licking and then tenderly nibbling at her nipples.

"Sweet Mother! I've never had such a beautiful build up as this before. Not even my late husband." She giggled. "No, especially not my late husband."

He touched her skirt but the caught his hand and pulled it away. "Not yet, sweetheart."

It was ten minutes more before he got her skirt off and then she wouldn't let him touch the silk drawers she wore.

"I'm not ready," she protested.

Spur rolled on top of her, spread her legs and lay on her crotch, humping slowly with his hips until her hips began to beat in rhythm with his. Then he unbuttoned the drawers, slid them down and she kicked them off her feet.

"Oh, yes!" she said. "Now I'm ready!"

He entered her gently, felt her hot response and they raced together to their first climax quickly.

As they lay in each other's arms in the afterglow, Evangeline kissed him and sighed, "At least a dozen more times!" she said. "Now that I'm in the mood I want to stay that way all night. Promise me you won't get tired and run out on me."

Spur promised.

"Let's talk about Doc. You have to let him stay here. The town needs him. I've been going to him once a month or so. What would any of us do without him?"

They talked about Doc for a half hour. Spur brought up all of the legal problems he had, and how Doc should go back just to clear his name.

"But he's got an excellent reputation right here in his new life. Why would he want to go back there? His wife and family are here. Three kids already. He's respected, loved, needed, right here in Johnson Corners."

Spur fixed them new drinks and changed the subject. "Since you're so good solving my problems, who is the counterfeiter here in town?"

"Who? Only one man could do it all, that's Bart Concord, our banker. Who else could spread fake money around so easily?"

"Could, is the right word, here. He could. But from what I've seen of him and what other people tell me, he isn't the kind of man who would do something like that. This little bundle of five dollar bills could put half the town into bankruptcy, make twenty families flat broke and out in the street."

Evangeline nibbled his ear. "So don't believe me. Are you rested up enough?"

"Rested enough for what?"

She hit him in the shoulder. "Another way, let's try it another way."

By midnight they had made love four times. Evangeline fixed them a midnight breakfast of hashbrowns, over easy eggs, toast and jam and lots of coffee.

Neither of them had bothered to dress. They ate over the small table and when the last of the food and coffee were gone Spur led her back to the bedroom.

"This time I want to be on top," Evangeline said. Spur grinned.

"Anywhere, anytime," he said. Spur knew he should be working on the case, somehow. He pushed it out of his mind. Tomorrow would be time enough. He felt the womanly soft body lowering on him and he jolted upward in delight.

They woke up a little after seven the next morning and Evangeline looked at Spur in surprise for a moment. Then a brilliant smile transformed her face into a feast of pleasures as she reached over and kissed Spur's chest.

He was up in a second, holding her on the bed.

"Hey, you got breakfast last night, my turn this morning. Let me prowl your ice box and your cupboard."

A half hour later he had breakfast ready, a stack of hotcakes, with hot syrup, half a dozen strips of bacon and two sunny side up eggs on top of the cakes. A big cup of coffee completed the meal.

For a small lady, Evangeline had a good appetite. He made two more flapjacks for her and then they settled down on the edge of the bed, still undressed, watching each other.

"That was the best night of lovemaking I've ever had, including my honeymoon!" Evangeline said. She laughed. "Do you have time for a couple more?"

Spur stroked her breasts, then kissed them before he shook his head. "I'd be a stretcher case before noon. And I do have some work to do. First a change of clothes, and then another talk with Doc, probably. Were you serious about picking the banker for the counterfeiter?"

"Absolutely. He's the only one in town I can think of who has the outlets for passing the bills. He simply puts in half bad fives when we ask for change or cash checks, or get a loan. It's perfect."

"Too perfect, that's why I don't believe it."

"If I'm right, you owe me a week's camping trip up the Little Blue River."

"Camping? You like to camp?"

"My favorite hobby. I go every summer. I have all the equipment."

"You're on. And if I win, you have to let me run the roulette wheel for a night downstairs, and keep all of my winnings."

"Deal."

Spur got dressed. She watched him, lying on the bed in a series of provocative and sexy poses, but she couldn't entice him into taking off his clothes.

"Business calls," he said. He left the dishes for her to wash and a messy kitchen, but kissed her long and with feeling when he was ready to go down the steps.

"Will I see you tonight, here, for supper?"

"Who will run the store?"

"Freddie, my number one man downstairs. He manages for me and is honest. First honest manager I've ever found. But I pay him well."

"Deal." Spur went out the door and down the steps. It was a little after nine when he walked into the hotel and found a note in his key box. He took it upstairs and was about to order bath water when he read the note. It was signed by "Princess."

"Mr. McCoy. I remembered the man. He doesn't come in a lot but for special occasions and he always wants me and sometimes I make an exception. This time was about three months ago, and he kept telling me how he had a money tree. Then he paid me with six five dollar bills. I didn't think anything of it. He is a good tipper.

"Now I see how he could afford it. The man is our banker, Bart Concord. He has to be the counterfeiter."

"I'll be damned," Spur McCoy said out loud.

18

Spur stared at the note from the madam and snorted. So the counterfeiter was the banker after all, if Princess's memory was right. He figured it was. So he had misread Concord. The country bumpkin had outjuggled him. He'd take care of that oversight as soon as the bank opened. No sense going in early and let him get suspicious.

Spur washed up, shaved and changed clothes. Things were starting to come together. But could Concord have done the whole thing by himself? He wondered.

He still had to decide about Doc Slocum. Doc should go back and face the charges and prove them wrong. But that would involve his first wife and child and his whole old way of life. He was settled here, was loved and needed. What more could a man ask for?

Still, the law said he had to go back.

Spur McCoy was the law out here. What he said,

what he did was the only law some of these folks saw in years.

He went down to the street and walked out of town on the Denver road. It was little more than a wagon track, but the stages maneuvered over it. Eventually there would have to be country road work done. But not for a few years.

Doc, what the hell was he going to do about Doc?

He walked out for half an hour trying to sort out everything he knew about the case, then turned and came back. He was on the outskirts of town when he saw a gray horse tied to a tree near some rocks. He heard a shot from behind the rocks and when he came closer he realized it was Willard Kleaner's mount.

Spur started to walk toward the horse when he heard another shot and then a scream. He ran for the rocks. Behind them he found Willard sprawled on the ground, a six-gun in the dirt and blood gushing from the boy's right upper thigh.

Spur pulled the boy's kerchief from around his throat and folded it into a compress and pushed it against the spurting blood. He stripped off his belt and cinched it up around the leg to hold the cloth in place over the wound.

"What happened?" Spur asked as he worked.

"Practicing my draw," Willard said through his pain. "I got mixed up and I guess I shot myself."

"I thought you agreed . . ." Spur stopped. The kid looked so chagrined, so hurting that Spur didn't have the heart to scold him.

Spur stuffed the boy's six-gun in his belt, picked him up carefully, protested the right thigh and began walking the quarter mile into town.

"I can ride," Willard said through gritted teeth.

"You ride six feet and that thigh will bust open again, then nobody could stop it. A man don't have to lose much blood to come up dead. Saw it happen too many times in the big war."

At the edge of town someone saw them and ran to bring Doc Slocum. A block from the medic's office the compress came off and blood spurted from the wound again.

"You must have hit a big artery in there, Willard," Spur said. He put the strapping youth on a patch of green grass on a lawn in front of a house and fumbled with the compress.

"Let me do that," a voice said over Spur's shoulder.

Doc Slocum knelt down beside Spur and his knowing hands began to examine the wound. He put on a fresh compress and held it in place slowing the blood flow. He put some white sticky tape over the compress to hold it.

"I can't do it here. That might hold until we get him to my office. Where's a cart?"

"Too slow," Spur said. "I'll carry him. You watch the wound."

Spur picked up Willard and carried him again. He took long swinging strides, almost running but keeping it smooth so Willard didn't jolt. A dozen people on the sidewalks watched as they hurried down Main Street to the doctor's office and inside.

The compress came off again and a spurt of blood shot out hitting Spur in the chest.

"Damnit!" Doc spouted. "We got to hurry!" He quickly cut a hole in a large piece of white cloth and put it over Willard with the hole over the wound. Then he used a fresh compress and held it with his hand. He had Spur hold the compress in place and

176

wrapped his belt around Willard's thigh and twisted it tight until it almost cut off the blood flow. Then he examined the wound again.

He repaired what damage he could, then stitched the sides of the bullet hole back together. Halfway through Willard sighed and passed out.

Doc finished, put a tight bandage over the wound after he had coated it with some salve, then put a second bandage over the first. He sat back and wiped the sweat off his forehead.

Spur sagged into a chair across the room.

"Damn good thing you came, Doc. He was bleeding like a throat-slit steer."

"Just routine. I get my share of gunshots. This one was strange, like it came from above, slanted down through the thigh and out almost at once."

"Accident, Doc. Willard shot himself learning how to draw."

"Damn fool kid."

"He never would have made it without you, Doc. I've seen too many men die of gunshot wounds not that bad. I couldn't get the bleeding stopped."

"Takes a little know-how is all." Doc looked embarrassed. "Help me get Willard into the recovery room, could you? He's grown half a hand since he got to town."

When Willard was safely tucked into bed in the next room, and a small woman brought in to watch him, Doc and Spur went into the doctor's office.

"Take off that shirt or it's ruined," Doc said. That was the first time Spur noticed the blood. Doc rinsed out the blood from the shirt in cold water, then used a little soap to get the last of the stain clean. He wrung out the wet shirt and hung it over a chair.

"I didn't know you did laundry, too, Doc."

"When a man's fighting for his life, McCoy, anything that helps, helps. You decided what to do about me yet?"

"Frankly . . . no. Like today, without you Willard would be dead by now. That helps. I'll decide soon."

Twenty minutes later Spur's light shirt was dry and he put it on. Doc Slocum was with a patient. Spur slipped out the side door and checked his vest. No blood on it. It hid most of the wrinkles in the just dry shirt.

A man ahead stared at Spur as he walked along the boardwalk. He turned and Spur tensed, his hand near his six-gun, but the man only rubbed his face.

"Say, are you that U.S. Marshal guy?"

"Close enough," Spur said.

"You just can't take away Doc Slocum. He done saved my right arm last winter. No doc here I'd have lost it sure. I was in a logging accident and Doc came out to the camp and stitched me back together again. Told me what to do and all. I'd be a one armed man by now if it warn't for him."

"Yes, thank you, I understand." Spur went past him and toward the hotel. He was stopped three more times on the street by men and women all urging him to let Doc stay in town.

At the hotel, a circle of a dozen women silently walked around the front steps. Each carried a stick with a sign on it. They all said, "Save our Doctor!" Spur saw them well down the street and circled the block and went in the back door and up to his room. He changed his shirt and checked his six-gun, then he went out the side door to see the banker. It was after ten by that time and the doors would be open.

Spur walked into the bank, saw the president's office door was open and went in. He closed the door behind him and stood in front of the modest desk, staring hard at Bart Concord.

"It's over, Concord. I'm from the United States Secret Service and I'm arresting you for counterfeiting five dollar bills and distributing them."

Concord leaned back in his chair. Surprise flooded his face, then slowly it crumpled. His shoulders sagged and he shook his head. "I told him it wouldn't last forever. Figured we'd get caught sometime. I was even starting to pull back some."

Spur sat down. "Tell me about it."

"Well it started about two years ago. This man I know said he could get an engraved plate for a five dollar bill. He knew I had a printing press. It's a hobby of mine. I print up all the forms for the bank, and my own stationery, things like that. At first I told him not a chance. I'm a banker, the honesty of the currency is a vital factor in my business. Counterfeit could ruin me.

"Then he pointed out that it might help, too. I could start making loans at low interest and without the usual collateral, so we could help out some struggling business firms. We could help people buy houses. All of this because we'd be using about half counterfeit for the actual cash we advanced.

"It took me several months to come around. In that time two businesses went broke that I could have saved. One man lost his house and shot himself leaving a wife and two children. At last I figured I'd do it. I would not make any profit from it, and it would be for the good of the town.

"By then this other man said he could get the plate, but I'd have to print up ten thousand dollars worth of the fives for him, and he would circulate them in Denver.

"By that time I was trapped. He said he'd go to the sheriff if I tried to back out. So, a month later I began experimenting with the press. My partner brought the paper from Denver. He said it was **almost exactly the same kind the Treasury Department** used to print the bills."

"Just who is this partner of yours, Concord."

The banker got up and walked to a closet, then came back. "I don't think I should tell you. He'd kill me for sure. He's told me as much."

"We'll get to that later. What happened next?"

"I got the press set right and the ink exactly the shade I needed and I printed off fifty. Just for fun I began passing them around town. Nobody knew the difference. I even checked with my two tellers who handle money all day. They couldn't tell the difference.

"Of course I never let them see two of the bills together. The serial numbers are a dead giveaway. My partner took fifty of them to Denver and passed them with no problems. People tend to trust a fiver more than they would a ten or a twenty. A twenty dollar bill is half a month's pay for most working men.

"After that I printed off five thousand worth for my partner and then two thousand for me. I began using it for special loans, I'd make. I kept two businesses afloat with those loans, and now they are solid and making money. I'm proud of that, McCoy, even if it might not have been entirely legal."

"Let's see the press, Concord."

The banker took him into a double locked back room where the platen printing press stood next to a window. There was a type case with six drawers of different fonts of hand set type of several sizes. A table held stacks of paper, and half a dozen bank forms were stacked on another table.

Spur looked at the forms. "You do good press work. Where is the plate?"

"It's not mine. My partner . . ."

"Who is this partner? You're going to have to tell me sometime. I guarantee that I'll protect you from him whoever he is."

"I realize that you'll try. He's a most forceful individual and quite frankly he frightens me."

"You should be more scared of me, Concord. I can put you into a federal prison for twenty years."

Concord wiped at moisture on his forehead. "I know that. This could hurt a lot of people. But . . . it doesn't have to. I've had a plan to pick up the bad money as it came into the bank in deposits. Most of the bills would be laundered out of the local system in about a year."

"The plate, Concord."

The banker sighed, went to the wall and pushed back a hidden panel and then lifted out a two-foot square section of the wall. Behind it was a safe. He twirled the knob, opened the door and took out a small package wrapped in a dozen layers of newspaper.

Inside was the metal engraved printing plate. Spur took it to the window and checked it against one of the fake bills. There was no doubt, it was the right plate. A small imperfection on the lower edge of the figure five, showed on both plate and bill.

Spur held the plate by both ends and slammed it against the edge of the window sill. The zinc plate broke neatly in half.

"Oh, God! I'm a dead man! He's going to kill me for sure now!"

"Who, Nevin Nelson?"

"Yes . . . how did you know?"

"I've been in town a while. So Nelson is the partner. He had the contacts in Denver, right?"

"Yes. Then once it got going he threatened to expose me to the sheriff, ruin me, close down my bank. I couldn't let that happen. All these good people *depend on me.*"

"Too bad their trust wasn't better placed. Concord, do you have any idea how many of the counterfeit bills you circulated in town?"

"Oh, yes, exactly. I keep records. So far the total is just a little over eight thousand four hundred. I haven't made any loans from the fake money for several months now."

"That's a lot of bills, Concord. How much have you printed for Nelson to take to Denver?"

"He kept pressuring me. He said he had to pay three thousand for the plate. So far it's up to a little over twelve thousand."

"It's over, you realize that?"

Concord slumped in a chair. "Yes, the printing is over. But I've had a plan all along to bring the bills back in. To go through the cash receipts every day and take out the bad bills and replace them with genuine ones."

Spur looked at him in surprise. He'd never caught a counterfeiter before who had any plans to make good on his bad bills. He was interested.

"Just how would that work, Concord?"

"Like I said. After the tellers went home, I'd go through their cash drawers and the receipts and deposits for the day and simply replace the bad bills with good ones from my private account."

"How long would it take?"

"To get them all? Never could. Some of them go out of town on the stage with visitors. Somebody might send a fiver in a letter home. But I figure I can capture about 95 percent of the bad bills in a little over a year."

Spur rubbed his jaw. It just might be worth it. It certainly would be better than jailing Concord and letting that eight thousand in counterfeit keep circulating or be called in and bankrupt some of the citizens.

"What would your partner say about this plan?"

"He'd kill me to save his own skin. Right now I think he suspects you're more than you told him."

"So my next move is to go see your good friend, Nevin Nelson the lawyer from Denver with the unsavory past."

"You heard about that?"

"Everyone has. First, do you have any more of the bad money printed?"

"Yes. I keep some on hand."

"How much?"

"About five thousand. That's a thousand bills. I keep them wrapped in ten stacks of a hundred each."

"Get them."

Concord went back to the safe and brought out the bundles of bills. Spur checked them. The serial numbers were identical.

"Damn fine engraving work, and printing. Too bad it was all illegal. You have a stove in here?"

Five minutes later they fed the last of the bills into the pot bellied heating stove in the storage room and Concord shook his head.

"Damn sad way to see my printing work come to its end this way."

"Better than stoking the furnace at the federal prison in Denver."

Spur made his decision quickly. "Concord, I'll trust you to do what you say you will. Tonight you begin laundering out the bad money. You have enough to cover it all?"

"I'll sell one building I own and that should cover what I'm short. You mean you'll really let me do it this way?"

"I don't see any value in ruining a lot of other folks lives for the mistakes you made. In the meantime you'll have a fine to pay to Uncle Sam and a lot of community service work to do here in town. I'll be through town from time to time to check up on you. I find any more funny money, your ass gets burned right into the nearest federal lockup!"

"No chance of that, Mr. McCoy. My only worry now is Nelson. How can you convince him to go along with this?"

"That's my problem, and it is a problem. That's my next visit. I'd suggest you stay in the bank and rest of the morning. You get set to clean up the five dollar population around Johnson Corners." Spur walked out of the bank. He had ten of the bad bills and the broken plate for evidence if he ever needed it. He hadn't decided if he'd even report this to his superiors.

19

Spur McCoy walked from the bank with a dozen thoughts churning through his head. He figured that Nevin Nelson was not the kind of man to take being arrested peacefully. He would come out fighting and clawing. The man might already be out of town running for his life.

No, Nelson was also the kind of man who would not run until he had to. So he would be here, in his office, waiting for Spur to call back on him for the estimate of the legal position of the Priscilla Davis property. And he was suspicious of Spur's motives.

Spur would find out soon enough where Nelson was.

Spur put his foot on the first wooden step leading upward toward the lawyer's office. He checked his .45 in its leather, and found it loose and ready. Spur walked up the steps and touched the lawyer's door. It was unlatched and swung open.

"Come in, McCoy," Nelson's voice said from

beyond the door. "Unlatched it just special for you."

Spur pushed open the door and stared at the business end of a sawed off shotgun, double barreled. The black muzzles gazed at him from just over the top of the lawyer's desk.

"Thought you'd be in to see me after your long talk with my little fat friend. Did he vomit up everything he knew? You are a lawman, right?"

McCoy watched the man's eyes, they were always the clue to a man with a gun. Nelson's were steady, hard, determined. He'd pull the trigger at the slightest movement of Spur's right hand toward his gun. Slowly McCoy lifted both hands until they were even with his head.

"Just came in to get that report I paid you for."

"Sure you did. Put your hands down slowly, then cross your arms in front. You move sudden and you're dead with buckshot. Now answer my question. You are a lawman or not?"

"You know I am or you wouldn't have that widow-maker in your hands. I'm here to pick up that thirteen thousand dollars in bogus five dollar bills you owe the U.S. Government."

"Figured as how. Now we have problem, you and I. How do I kill you so nobody knows it was me? At least nobody except fat Concord can know and he don't matter a tinker's damn."

Nelson scowled at Spur for a moment, then lifted from the chair slowly, keeping the shotgun centered at the lawman's chest.

"Not an inch. I don't want to see any part of you move more than a quarter of an inch or you'll get blown in half with both barrels. Ever seen a man shot this close with a scattergun? Not pretty, but that wouldn't bother you. You'd already be in hell stoking the furnaces.''

As he talked, Nelson moved slowly around the desk, to the side of Spur, then behind him. The Secret Service Agent saw it all, including the six-gun in Nelson's belt.

There was simply no chance, no way to try to draw against the aimed and cocked shotgun. He'd be dead before his hand touched iron.

So he waited.

As Nelson edged sideways behind Spur and out of sight, the lawman figured what was coming. It came quicker than he expected, the stunning, blow to the back of his head by the butt of the pistol, setting off a dozen brilliant flashes in his head. He tried to swing around to defend himself somehow.

But it was too late, the signal wires controlling his shoulders and arms shorted out and then his legs went and he tried to catch himself as he fell forward, missing the desk but slamming his forehead into the wooden floor with a jolt.

By that time Spur never felt the fall. He was unconscious.

Over him, Nelson grinned.

''Not such a big shot government agent now, are you, Spur McCoy? Only problem is what to do with you. Has to be the back way. Damn, wish I had one of those new steamer trunks. I could carry you down the back stairs, but you're a big one.''

Spur had fallen on his six-gun. Nelson used his foot to roll him over, then pulled out the long barreled weapon and snorted. He put it in a desk drawer, then used strong twine and tied Spur's hands behind him, then his ankles together.

''Time to call in a few favors,'' Nelson said softly.

He went out his front door and down two offices to the third one and talked for a moment with a big man behind a desk. The man had a thick beard and hair longer than the fashion. He belched, nodded and followed Nelson back to his office.

"He'd be a heap easier to move if he was already dead," the shaggy man said. "I could use my knife right now."

"No, for God's sakes, man, use your head. That would leave blood stains all over the place. You should be that smart. We untie him and both of us help him down the back steps and into a buggy. Then when he's out of sight we tie him up again and take him for a nice long ride he won't come back from. Even you should be able to understand that, Quint."

"Yeah, sure I can. Let's move him."

They dragged him by the shoulders to the back door, then Nelson looked up. There was a small porch-like passage along the three offices to the steps at the far end.

"Untie him now," Nelson said. They cut the twine and lifted Spur upright. He was a dead weight.

"We'll put him between us, arms over our shoulders. We can carry him that way and it'll look like he's drunk."

Nelson went back for Spur's hat and jammed it down low on his head half covering his face. "That helps."

They positioned Spur between them and opened the door. Someone was going down the last of the steps. They waited. When he left they moved out on the passage. Spur's feet dragged along. They talked to each other, looked at Spur, pretending he was drunk. Nobody paid any attention to them.

One woman looked out a back window and then quickly away. At the stairs they were so narrow one man had to go first, so the three of them were sideways on the steps.

"Damn this is hard," Quint said. He was the man above Spur.

"Shut up and get it done," Nelson whispered. "And be sure you remember how to use that Colt in your belt when you get outside of town a ways. I don't want him found for a long time, you understand that?"

Before Quint could respond, Spur came alive in their arms. He lashed out with his left foot, jamming it in Nelson's side and ramming him down the last six steps so he landed in a heap at the bottom. Spur swung his free right hand, jolting his fist into the surprised Quint's jaw. He was driven back a step. Spur's left hand came free of Quint and he slammed his left fist deep into the unprotected belly before him. Quint yelled and sat down on the steps, his eyes glassy.

Spur powered one more right fist into Quint's face, sending him into dream land. Quickly Spur grabbed the six-gun from Quint's belt and spun. He saw Nelson pawing for the gun at his belt as he ran around the corner of the building heading down the short end of the alley.

Spur leaped down the remaining steps and ran after Nelson. McCoy's slashed at blood that ran into his right eye from the wound on his forehead. He got around the building and listened to a slug crash into the wall beside him.

Missed.

Thirty yards ahead. Nelson had stopped to take aim, now he sprinted on down the alley. Spur ran after him. He turned at the end of the alley toward Main. That meant more people, less chance for a good shot.

Spur took the corner around the hardware store at the alley mouth wide, felt the whisper of hot lead lancing through the air just over his head, and surged ahead as Nelson darted across Main and vanished into a haberdashery.

A woman looked at the blood pouring down Spur's face and fainted in front of the grocery. Spur dashed across the street to the men's clothing store and paused at the door. He heard nothing inside so darted in, exposing himself for a second in the light of the door.

A pistol round exploded sharply in the confines of the small store, but the slug ripped through only fabric as it cut a double hole in Spur's pants leg.

McCoy came with his borrowed gun up, cocked and ready but he found only a frightened store owner flat on the floor behind a counter pointing at the rear of the store.

Spur pushed open the door slowly from a crouch, let one shot sing through the opening, then he rushed in. The back door was ajar. He ran to it and looked out. He saw Nelson running away but getting tired. Spur threw two shots at the figure and saw one round hit his shoulder. Nelson staggered, turned and fired two more rounds from his weapon, then it clicked on empty.

He carried it as he ran across the alley into a back yard and on through it.

Spur pushed three more rounds from the loops in his gun belt into his borrowed .45 as he ran. It gave him six shots if he had the chance.

Nelson was wounded and kept running. That meant the chase would be a long one. Spur knew he had to keep the man off a horse. The house on this side of the street had no shed, but the two on the other side of the street did.

Horses!

Spur ran faster, wiped some of the blood off his face and cleaned his left hand on his pants leg. He heard a horse nicker, and then saw Nelson in the other yard, trying to mount a horse.

Spur sent a shot over his head.

"Hold it, right there, Nelson. No way you can get past me."

"Dead or alive, I'm going to try."

A woman came out of the back of the house, saw Nelson on the horse, then Spur with the gun. She lifted a shotgun wavering between aiming at Spur and Nelson who had mounted now.

"Put down that six-gun, mister, or I'll dust you off with birdshot. You on my Bessie, get down nice and easy."

Nelson ignored her, dug his heels into the horse and slammed forward, the only way he could go, directly at Spur.

The woman lifted the barrel and fired the first round over her horse's head, then turned and aimed at Spur. He dove for the ground behind the end of a low rock wall just as the buckshot peppered the rocks and the ground around him.

A half a second later the bay horse leaped over the wall directly over Spur and galloped away to the south. Spur jumped up but the pair was already out of pistol range.

"Ma'am, I'm a law officer, I'd like to borrow a horse to chase this outlaw. You have another one saddled?"

"You that McCoy guy?"

"Yes, ma'am and a wanted outlaw is getting away."

"Why didn't you say so? Philip is saddled and ready." She ran to the shed and brought out a big black. "Philip will outrun Bessie any day. Here. You want the scatter gun?"

Spur mounted, then took the shotgun and ten shells she had in her apron pocket.

"Much obliged. I'll bring back both your horses."

Spur kicked the black in the flanks and he jolted forward, then settled down to a steady cantor until Spur urged him into a gallop toward the fast vanishing bay ahead of them.

An hour later Spur settled down to playing a game of cat and mouse with Nelson. He knew the territory. He had led Spur into a series of small valleys and ridges, hiding now and then, but having to show himself to cross the next narrow opening.

The man running had the advantage. At every bit of cover there were always two directions he could take. The hunter had to wait to see which direction his quarry went before he could follow.

Then Spur saw something ahead that gave him hope. Nelson had made the turn that meant soon he would wind into a box canyon. It ended in a sheer rock wall of no more than twenty feet, but impossible to ride out of. Nelson might be able to climb out, but at least it would hold him up.

Spur cut across country, losing sight of Nelson for a few minutes, cutting off two valleys, and coming into a position where his man would have to come out of the last ridge and plunge across a hundred yard wide valley.

The cleared area was knee deep in waving green grass fed by the winter snows and its spring melt off. Spur waited under a fully leafed aspen that hid him entirely.

Five minutes later, Nelson came out of the edge of the cover on the far side. He looked behind, then rode hard across the open stretch.

He came within ten yards of where Spur figured he would dash back into cover, hoping this time not to have been seen. As Nelson came into the darkness from the light he was momentarily blinded.

Spur was ready. Nelson stopped five yards into the woods to let his eyes adjust. Spur had the pistol up with a two handed grip and aimed at Nelson's chest. The round went wide, smashed into Nelson's good shoulder, slamming him off the horse and screaming on the ground.

Spur rode up quickly, but Nelson was gone. The Secret Agent quieted his horse and listened. A boot broke a twig to the left. Spur moved his horse that way and found Nelson behind a two foot thick lodgepole pine.

He held up his pistol and aimed it at Spur.

"You're out of rounds, remember?"

"I had a pocket full. I planned ahead. Get down from your horse and take off your boots."

Spur fired a round between the man's feet. He jumped back.

"I'm not fooling. I have six shots left. You're a dead man."

Spur could see in the chambers of the weapon now. There was no dull reflection of lead inside any of them. Chances were the one under the hammer was also empty.

"So shoot. I'm waiting."

Blood stained Nelson's left arm. His right wrist seemed broken the way he held it. He stared at Spur a moment, then threw the empty weapon at him and ran into the thick brush.

For five minutes Spur herded a tired Nelson, moving him back toward his horse. Once Spur fired the shotgun over Nelson's head.

"Go ahead, kill me!" he raved. "I'm not going to any goddamn jail. That would be worse than dead."

They were in an open stretch where Nelson had nothing to hide behind. He picked up a four foot branch and swinging it as a club, charged Spur on the black.

Spur skittered the black backward out of reach.

"Put down the club, Nelson."

The man charged again, whacking the horse on the forelegs but there was little force in the blow. The horse screamed and ran off ten yards before Spur got him under control.

Spur moved back to the counterfeiter.

"Drop it or I'll shoot," Spur said. Nelson charged. Spur fired at his legs. The second slug hit one leg, but Nelson kept coming. The next round triggered before Spur could stop it found Nelson falling from the first hit.

The second slug hit him squarely in the face, just left of his right eye. He was dead by the time he hit the forest floor and rolled over on his back.

An hour later, Spur had dumped Nelson's body off the bay in front of the sheriff's office, then returned the two horses to the woman who owned them along with the shotgun and nine shells.

Back at the Sheriff's Office he told the sheriff he had wanted to question Nelson in connection with a counterfeiting case. The victim had drawn down on him, slugged him and was in the process of trying to kill him when he escaped and knocked out a man called Quint, and pursued the victim who refused to surrender.

The sheriff wrote down Spur's statement, had him sign it and then shook his head.

"We had a right nice and quiet town before you arrived. Are there going to be any more bodies dumped around here in the near future?"

"Won't be my doing if there are," Spur said. "My business here is almost finished."

"You got your man?"

"Yes, indeed, Sheriff. I got him."

"What about Doc Slocum?"

"That I'll let you know about tomorrow. First I have to go over to the doctor's office and get some minor surgery done on my scalp."

"Good luck. Doc might just decide to stitch up your mouth while he's at it!"

20

Ronald Lewton had been pacing in front of the sheriff's office for ten minutes when Spur came out. His anger had been building all the time and when he saw the Secret Service Agent, he flew at him with his arms waving.

"Why in the world did you encourage the boy to buy the gun? You should be ashamed of yourself! You almost got him killed. Then what would you have done? I know, I saw you teaching him with the rope. You undoubtedly suggested he buy the gun that he shot himself with."

Spur held up his hands but when that did no good he shouted.

"Hold it! Stop, right now! It's a little late for you to start showing some concern for the boy. You work him eight hours a day without paying him, you take his monthly stipend from his estate, and you treat him like poor relation.

"What in hell is the matter with you?"

Lewton dropped his hands. His face worked and tears seeped from his eyes. His shoulders sagged and all at once he was crying. Tears flowed down his cheeks. He sobbed and then furiously tried to stop.

"I . . . I . . . I guess I'm angry at myself. You're right. I've not appreciated the boy. He's smart and bright, he's a good boy. I'm sorry I accused you about the gun."

"I saw it. He showed it to me. I told him to put it away. He said he would. It must have been too much of a temptation. You know he's safe now. Doc Slocum saved his life."

"I'd guess you did too, carrying him into town that way."

"Had to be done. Now I need to let the sawbones take care of my head."

"Oh, land sakes, McCoy! Didn't notice. That's quite a gouge out of your forehead. It's bleeding again. You best get that fixed up right soon."

"On my way." Spur continued down the boardwalk toward the medical office. He was just past Priscilla Davis's store when he heard someone behind him. He turned and saw Priscilla there running toward him. She had a frown on her face and when she came closer he saw she was terribly upset.

He stopped and turned toward her. Priscilla was only four feet away when she lifted her right hand and he saw the gun. Before he could move she fired three times.

Spur dove to the left, rolled into the alley and pressed against the side of the building. He should be dead. The muzzle had been centered on his chest when she fired all three times.

Priscilla screamed and raced into the alley after him. She looked at the wrong side first and Spur leaped across the opening and caught her from behind and slapped the weapon from her hand. He spun her away and picked up the gun from the dust.

A minute later Sheriff Phillip Gump ran into the alley. Spur had broken open the weapon, an Adams Pocket Revolver. The fancy little .32 caliber weapon had gold inlay on the barrel, cylinder and body.

"McCoy, you all right?" Sheriff Gump asked.

"Guess so. Don't seem to be bleeding anywhere now."

"Look at the rounds."

Spur did as the sheriff suggested. They were blanks. Regular cartridges but with rounds of cardboard stuffed in where the lead slug should be and sealed with wax.

"You know about Priscilla?"

"Nearly everybody in town does. Too bad nobody told you. She's usually harmless enough. When she takes a fancy to a man and he doesn't return the affection, she gets downright unhappy and dangerous."

"I know. The first time her pistol had rounds with lead slugs in them. She barely missed me."

"Sorry, McCoy. I usually check her guns once a week and put in blanks. She doesn't remember. Guess I slipped up."

McCoy laughed. "Sheriff, I'm just glad she got this Adams with the blanks. Otherwise you'd be setting up a funeral right now. Who taught this lady to shoot?"

"Don't know. Her daddy, probably. She kind of went to pieces after he died. Some people say she and her father had what we call an unnatural relationship. At least he kept her satisfied sexually and in line. Last four or five years have been right lively when Priscilla gets her dander up."

Spur looked at the woman. She leaned against the wall in the alley, staring into the street. She paid no attention to them. A moment later she lifted her skirts delicately to keep them out of the dust and dirt, walked daintily to the boardwalk and vanished down the block.

"She don't even remember what happened," Sheriff Gump said. "Sad case. She's such a pretty woman. No man around here will go anywhere near her. Not even with that gold mine of a store she owns thrown in."

Spur handed the fancy little gun to the sheriff. "Better reload this one and put it back where she keeps her weapons. Hope the next guy in town has a warning."

"Guess I could meet each stage and tell folks, but somehow I don't have the time, and it seems a little cruel. She hasn't even wounded anyone so far."

"Glad I didn't break her record. Now I better get down to Doc Slocum's before my head starts bleeding again."

"Have you decided . . ."

"No, Sheriff Gump. When I decide what to do about Doc, everyone will know." He turned and walked down to the boards and on toward the medical office.

He made one stop at the Moon General Store and asked if they had magazines and books. They had a few in the back corner. Spur made his purchase and left with it in a brown wrapper.

Doc Slocum snorted when he saw him.

"Wouldn't let me fix you up when you was here,

would you? Contrary cuss if I ever saw one. Now sit down and be quiet so I can get the blood off you and then maybe you'll stop scaring our little old ladies. Hear you made one faint already today and got shot full of cardboard by another one."

"You knew about Priscilla? Why didn't you tell me?"

"Didn't know you were sinning with her. Man's got a right to some privacy."

"In this case privacy could have got me killed."

"Couldn't have happened to a more deserving gent."

"Don't be mad just because you never made the wanted posters, Doc. I could solve that for you by sending a telegram to Washington. They'd print me up a good one. Make the reward two dollars. If you were in good health."

"Quiet while I spread some whiskey over your head."

"Usually I take it internally."

"Not this time."

"You're still mad at me. Furious, I'd guess. Sheriff Gump said you might stitch my mouth shut."

"Damn fine idea."

He used a cloth and washed off the gash in Spur's forehead, then splashed it with alcohol from a bottle.

Spur jolted sideways. "Damn! I like it better in my mouth."

"Later."

"Hear you have three kids, Doc."

"True. Roots. People like roots."

"What in hell am I going to tell Washington?"

"Lie. They won't believe the truth."

Doc put some salve on the wound, which wasn't as

deep as it looked, and taped it together. He put a bandage over it and washed his hands.

"You'll be good as new in a year or two. I tried to leave it so you'll have a big scar."

"Thanks, Doc. Now where is Will? I've got something for him."

"Right where we put him, second door down. He's got visitors."

When Spur opened the door he saw Ron Lewton and his wife sitting by Willard's bed. They looked up as he came in.

"Hi, Cowboy," Spur said. "Won't take up much of your time."

"Hi, Mr. McCoy. I got lots of time. Doc says I got to stay here for two more days, then at home for a week again before I start walking much. Something about part of me growing back together."

"Good, keep you out of trouble. Oh, brought you something to make the time go by." Spur handed him the small sack and stepped back.

Willard eagerly opened the paper and took out three Western dime novels. His eyes glowed as he looked at them.

"Wow, look at this Aunt Zelda! The latest ones! *Kid Rodeo and the Silver Moon,* and another one, *Sharpshooters at Rimrock Ranch,* and this one, *Rustlers on the Circle K.* Wow! I'll have enough to keep me reading for more than two days. Thanks Mr. McCoy!"

"It's going to cost you."

"Easy, I can pay for them. Uncle Ronald says I get to keep the twenty dollars a month from my inheritance."

"That's fine, Will, but this is a different kind of cost. You have to put that six-gun away in your uncle's hotel safe and leave it there until you're eighteen. You have no need for a pistol and it can only get you in more trouble.''

''Yeah, I guess you're right. But in *Six-Guns and Rustlers*, this fifteen year old kid . . .'' He stopped and grinned. ''Yeah, that's just a story written by some guy in Chicago or New York who has never been west of the Mississippi.''

They all laughed.

Zelda brought up a package and pushed it on the bed.

''I brought you some of your things, Willard,'' she said softly. She hadn't had a drink all morning.

Willard opened the sack and grinned. ''Four of my Western novels! Great. Now I can compare them. Thanks!'' He reached out and hugged his aunt who was slightly embarrassed.

Spur waved. ''I have one more job to do. Don't like it, but I have to do it. You get well now and concentrate on your riding and roping. That's what a cowboy needs to do. When you get good enough, I bet your uncle could arrange for you to stay on one of the ranches for a couple of months next summer and learn to be a real cowhand.''

When Spur left, Willard and his uncle were talking about the possibilities.

Spur took a deep breath, felt the blood pounding in his wounded forehead and went to the street. He heard the noise before he opened the outer door. It sounded like a marching band.

Just outside the office door he stopped short. There were a hundred people there standing silently. Now they all looked at him. The sounds had come from an undermanned German Oom Pah band. A man in the front of the crowd held up his hand and the band stopped its brassy sound.

"Spur McCoy. This delegation is here to make damn sure that you don't take away our only doctor. Don't know how much of a Western man you are. A good doctor is one reason most folks stayed here in Johnson Corners. Means the town is going to survive and grow and a place we can put down roots and establish a family and a good life.

"Ain't a big town, yet. But Doc Slocum is helping it grow, helping us stay healthy, and takes care of us when we get sick or hurt. Hear that young Will wouldn't have made it if Doc hadn't been here ready.

"Lots of others would be six feet under right now, except for Doc. We know you think he done wrong back East. We don't give a tinker's damn about back East. We are here and Doc is here and we want him to stay.

"We think you got the wrong charges or the wrong man. Anyway, anything he might have done has been more than paid for by all the good he's done out here.

"Oh, one last thing. We believe in law and order, but sometimes it takes a local militia to settle matters. We got about fifty guns here right now, all legally deputized by Sheriff Gump to form a posse. We don't aim to let anybody take Doc Slocum out of town. Not even you.

"That's it, McCoy. That's where we stand."

Spur pushed his low crowned brown hat back on his head. The sun glinted off the Mexican silver pesos on the headband.

"Good people of Johnson Corners. Let me make

one thing clear. Fifty guns, or a thousand guns, wouldn't persuade me to leave Doc Slocum here.'' There was a rumble of anger from the crowd. Spur hurried on.

"**Ten thousand guns wouldn't do the job, not if I** knew he should be taken back to Washington, D.C. to face charges. However, I have investigated the case completely, and have determined that this man is not guilty of anything more than being afraid. And I ask, are there any of us who haven't been afraid of something at one time or another?''

"What I'm saying is that I'm not going to take Doc Slocum away. As far as I'm concerned, he's a free man!''

There were shouts of joy. The German band struck up and a dozen people began a square dance in the street. Bells rang, a dozen men fired pistols into the air and there was a swarm of people on the boardwalk to shake Spur's hand. As soon as he could, he slipped away through the throng and worked his way to the Evangeline Saloon and Gaming House. He went through the front door and took a cold bottle of beer that Evangeline held out for him.

She took his hand and led him to her table. The saloon was just open and only two card players were there. She put her small white hand over his large browner one.

"Thanks, McCoy. Thanks for letting Doc Slocum stay in town.,''

"No thanks needed, but you're welcome. Like I said, he was innocent. Why disrupt the lives of six or eight people so he can prove it? I'll dream up something to put the whole case to rest.''

"That's after our camping trip.''

"Oh, damn."

"I did win our bet didn't I? I bet that the counterfeiter was our banker Bart Concord. He's the one, right?"

"Oh, damn."

"You said that. Isn't he the bogus bills man?"

"Yes. He's the one."

"Good, you did lose the bet. We go camping up the Little Blue River for a week. I told you I have enough gear for two."

"Won't people talk?"

"They do now. Saloon owner is the same as saloon girl which is the same as *puta*, whore, prostitute, fancy lady. I've already been painted that way, I guess it's about time I start getting some of the good stuff that goes along with the name."

"You're not a naughty lady."

"Thanks for the support. What am I, a loose woman?"

"A wonderful woman, and as I remember, excitingly tight!"

Her glance came up quickly and she grinned. "A gentleman wouldn't have said that."

"Sometimes it's no fun to be a gentleman." He sipped his beer.

"I bet you haven't had dinner yet. It's almost noon. Let's go upstairs and I'll show you I can cook."

She took his hand and led him past the bar to the rear door and up the stairs to her apartment.

"I don't care who is watching," she whispered.

In the kitchen he turned a straight backed chair around and sat on it as he watched her.

"This camping trip, could we work in some fishing and a little hunting?"

"Might, if you cooperate."

"Oh. I'm good at that. I'm wondering about the accommodations. This equipment you have, does it include blanket rolls?"

"Of course. You won't have to sleep under fir boughs to stay warm."

"Good, good. The blanket rolls. Are they for one or made for two people?"

She finished slicing potatoes into a skillet and grinned. "I'd say that also depends on how you play your cards."

"Oh. I'd think I could play them just about anyway the dealer wanted them played."

"Good. Now, you never did tell me the details about our banker friend. I know you had a long talk with him this morning. My guess is that he confessed. Right?"

He told her what happened and how it was extremely important to keep it quiet.

"Concord will pick up all of the five dollar bill forgeries gradually, and the general public will know nothing about it. The only people in town who know have promised to keep it quiet so there won't be a panic, and so nobody will go bankrupt or lose his house or savings."

Twenty minutes later they sat down to a meal of fresh fried potatoes and onions and cheese, fresh peas and hot buttered sweet corn on the cob.

"I hope your camp cooking is this good," he said.

"Depends what the hunter and fisherman brings me to cook," she said. Then she stood. "Now there's something else I want to talk to you about that we didn't quite get to last night. It's in the bedroom."

"I have a headache," Spur said.

"Good. I have just the right kind of intense physical exercise to cure it."

"You're sure?"

"Positive."

"I may need more than one treatment."

"We have a week to see if the cure will work."

Spur McCoy smiled. "Sounds fair to me," he said and they hurried into the bedroom.

Make the Most of Your Leisure Time
with
LEISURE BOOKS

Please send me the following titles:

Quantity	Book Number	Price
_____	_____	_____
_____	_____	_____
_____	_____	_____
_____	_____	_____
_____	_____	_____

If out of stock on any of the above titles, please send me the alternate title(s) listed below:

_____	_____	_____
_____	_____	_____
_____	_____	_____
_____	_____	_____

Postage & Handling _____

Total Enclosed $_____

☐ Please send me a free catalog.

NAME _____
(please print)

ADDRESS _____

CITY _____ STATE _____ ZIP_____

Please include $1.00 shipping and handling for the first book ordered and 25¢ for each book thereafter in the same order. All orders are shipped within approximately 4 weeks via postal service book rate. PAYMENT MUST ACCOMPANY ALL ORDERS.*

*Canadian orders must be paid in US dollars payable through a New York banking facility.

Mail coupon to: **Dorchester Publishing Co., Inc.**
6 East 39 Street, Suite 900
New York, NY 10016
Att: ORDER DEPT.